First Round Lottery Pick

First Round Lottery Pick

Franklin White

www.urbanbooks.net

Urban Books, LLC
78 East Industry Court
Deer Park, NY 11729

First Round Lottery Pick ©copyright 2010 Franklin White

ISBN 13: 978-1-60162-212-9
ISBN 10: 1-60162-212-0

First Printing March 2010
Printed in the United States of America

10 9 8 7 6 5 4 3 2 1

This is a work of fiction. Any references or similarities to actual events, real people, living, or dead, or to real locales are intended to give the novel a sense of reality. Any similarity in other names, characters, places, and incidents is entirely coincidental.

Distributed by Kensington Publishing Corp.
Submit Wholesale Orders to:
Kensington Publishing Corp.
C/O Penguin Group (USA) Inc.
Attention: Order Processing
405 Murray Hill Parkway
East Rutherford, NJ 07073-2316
Phone: 1-800-526-0275
Fax: 1-800-227-9604

Dedication

The author dedicates this book to Frank Tatum,
Terry Poindexter, and Ralph White.

Acknowledgments

Big shout-outs go out to my family. Family knows who they be!

Let's all acknowledge, only 50% of black children enrolled in public schools in our country graduated last year. Let's also acknowledge, only 39% of all black males enrolled in our schools graduated last year. We should acknowledge and change the fact there are more black males in prison than college. Finally, let's acknowledge, too many children have never sat down at the dinner table with their mother and father at the same time to break bread. Let's acknowledge that this is unacceptable and needs to change. Real talk.

—Franklin

Chapter One

On and Poppin'

Except for the time we lived in a cardboard box, I had spent every day of my life in Poindexter Village. Rumor has it that a long time ago, an old man full of liquor renamed our housing project "The Vil," and that's where I grew up. It didn't take long to realize that drugs, crime, and everything else common to living in poverty was going to be a part of my life.

In The Vil, unemployment was always high, there wasn't a lot of money for nice things, practically no fathers were ever seen, and young pregnant girls were running around, trying to figure out who the fathers of their unborn kids were.

I was lucky. I stayed away from what the hood had to offer. I had no choice. It was the direction my mother moved me in while she tried to hold down a job. I spent most of my time on the basketball court with the old heads who would let me bounce my plastic ball on the side as they lived out their "Jordan dreams."

As a teenager all of a sudden, I started to grow like a weed and really begin to enjoy playing basketball. Then I made the AAU team. Next thing you know, I was the star of my high school team and the number one recruit in the nation.

With all I had accomplished, there weren't many times I could remember walking out our broken, squeaky screen door with a smile on my face while on my way to school. I didn't when my team won the state championship or when I got selected to play in the all-American game on ESPN, but Friday morning I knew I was showing all the teeth in my mouth, because I had made a decision. I was happy and speaking to anyone who crossed my path without looking out the corner of my eye to see if they meant me any harm as they walked by.

As I walked past the courts I had played on every day since I was four years old, not even all the empty beer cans, used condoms, or broken pint bottles of whiskey could change how I felt. It was hard not to focus on the rim of my first dunk, a thunderous one-handed tomahawk slam right in the face of the self-proclaimed king of courts in The Vil. I damn near broke his arm, and I was only in seventh grade. When I came back down to the ground, everyone stopped and looked at me like I was some type of freak of nature or something. I felt like King Kong. It was a sweet moment that I would never forget.

My memories quickly ceased just as I stepped off the curb into the street. The sound of screeching tires and the front end of a car were much too close to be funny and brought me back to reality.

"Whooo! Did you see that! Them brakes workin' like a son of a bitch! What's up, baby? Did you piss yourself or what?" Jalen shouted out at the top of his voice from behind the wheel of his car.

I looked down at his car again, and it was even closer to my body than I thought. "Jalen, I'm goin' to whup your ass. I still don't understand why your mother didn't give you up after birth, with your stupid ass."

Jalen was my partner in crime. Like a brother, we were joined at the hip, and I trusted him with my life, even though he played too damn much. As usual his music was bumping, and the song "I'm So Hood" was in everyone's ear.

Jalen slammed his car into park and, in one fluid motion, maneuvered his five feet nine inches, 160 pound frame from under the steering wheel and onto the door. He propped his head into his hand as he leaned on the hood and displayed a wide smile. "Now tell me again. Why yo' mama named you Langston, son?"

"Don't worry about my name, fool. You better watch yourself, with your non-driving skills." I took another glance in his car. "Besides, the only thing you *really* need to be talking to me about is why *my* girl is in the car with you." It was easy for me to notice Tori's eyes as she sat low in the front seat, bouncing her head to the hard bass. I could spot her anywhere because that's just how we flowed.

"'Cause, she's my girl now!" Jalen yelled back over his music.

Tori showed why I was feeling her the way I was. She jumped right in on Jalen. "You lying and your breath stank. Ain't that the way yo' mama and them used to say it." She began to tug and push at Jalen's passenger door a few times, but no matter how hard she pushed, it wouldn't open. "Boy, you better let me out this car. What you need to do is let MTV and Xzibit pimp this thing out!"

"Ain't nobody touching my car. It's a classic. Give up the respect. Just scoot back then kick out. You know how we do."

Jalen's car really was a wreck, but I still loved it. It was bad enough he didn't have a key and had to start it with a screwdriver underneath the hood some crazy way while someone stepped on the gas when they heard the car crank. Jalen's car had been our transportation since the first time he got it to run when he wasn't even supposed to be driving in the ninth grade.

I walked over to his Impala and yanked the car door about three times before it finally opened.

Tori stepped out and quickly reminded me why she was my girl. "What's up, *papi*? We stopped by to pick you up, but Reecy told us you were walking today. What's up with that?"

When Tori put her arm around my waist, I leaned back a bit and peeped her apple bottom stuffed inside her Azzure jeans.

"You better not let his mama hear you call her Reecy. You better school your girl, *L*."

"Jalen, would you shut up? My mother only smacks the taste out of *your* mouth when you call her Reecy. Look, let Tori drive into school so we can chat."

"Are you crazy? Tori ain't getting behind the wheel of my whip!"

Tori looked up at me. "Why? Why don't we all roll together like we always do? You know we don't have too many days to go anyway before graduation. We have to keep this thing gutter, baby."

"I need to talk to my boy for a minute."

"About what?"

"C'mon, Tori. Do this for me, a'ight."

Tori was disappointed, but it only made her look even better. Her lips were so juicy and sparkling with lip gloss, I wanted to kiss her right then and there. It wasn't a secret. I had the finest female at East High School. Tori was mixed and stirred up with blackness from her father's side of the family and some oriental spices from her mother. An easy five feet six inches and weighing no more than 125-pounds, her body was all there, and to top it off, she had a 4.0 grade point average. Not to mention, she was a virgin, and claimed it without any regrets despite the haters.

"Yeah, okay, I'll drive, but I'm telling you, if this car cuts off on me, I'm leaving it where it stops. Bet that." Tori walked over to the driver's side of the car, pushed Jalen out the way, then jumped in and drove off.

Jalen kept a close watch as she rolled down the street. "Ahh, damn! I forgot my smokes."

"You need a break anyway."

"Whatever, Langston. I'm telling you, man, if she wrecks my wheels—"

"Chill, man, let's just walk."

"You must be trippin'. You got me out here walking on my brand-new Js. What are you so serious for today, out here walking like we back in the day or something?"

"Because it's time to get serious."

"Serious? What's that supposed to mean?"

"I'm going pro, man. I'm putting my name in the draft."

"L, you know you can't play any pro ball until you do one year of college."

"Forget that, man. I'm talking about overseas. I'm going to do a three-year deal."

Jalen looked up at me. "Don't be playing, L. If you kicked game like that, this place would be in straight pandemonium. Don't you know?"

"Yeah, I know. So they better get ready, 'cause it's time."

"Why you change your mind all of a sudden? When I mentioned it after you blasted South for sixty-three points and fifteen rebounds."

"And twelve assists," I reminded him. "Don't forget the dishes, my brother. It makes the player."

"I know your stats, man. I just want to know how you came to the conclusion of going pro all of a sudden. Playing overseas ain't no place to fool around with."

I stopped walking. "Jalen, look at me. Does it look like I'm playing? I mean, why not? All the trades think I should. More pro scouts than college have been out to my games. Trust me, man; I think this is the right thing to do."

Jalen took a deep breath, almost like he was about to get upset with me. "Aww . . . L, tell me you didn't sign with that money-grubbing agent." He stopped and kicked a crack vial out of his way. "I'm so tired of that dude stressing me to get to you."

"Jalen, what do you take me for, man? I wouldn't sign with an agent. If I don't get drafted high enough in their draft, I'm going to Ohio State."

Jalen didn't look too pleased with that decision. "Psst! Well, let's hope you get drafted sky high 'cause Ohio State ain't never showed no love for b-ballers from this side of town since Granville Waiters.

"It don't matter."

"Why?"

"'Cause I'm going to get taken number one anyway."

"Get out of here. How do you know that?"

"I got a call last night."

"From who?"

I put my arm around Jalen. "Barcelona, my brother. They say, if I enter their draft, they are taking me *número uno*, baby!"

Jalen stopped walking again and looked up at me. I think he had tears in his eyes. He turned around and looked back to the courts where we both spent our days as young bucks. No doubt, he went back to the time when we were six-year-olds. I would shoot, and he would ride his bike with one training wheel up and down the court, telling me I could do better.

I had to push him out of his daze. "Man, you all right?"

"Yeah, man, this is crazy. I guess dreams do come true, don't they?"

"Oh, you ain't seen nothing yet, 'cause it's on and poppin'."

Chapter Two
Tight, ain't it?

That morning we took our time getting to school. After all, even though I would from time to time sit around and talk Jalen's ear off about the possibilities of going pro after college, actually having the chance within reach was like waking up in a whole different world. I hadn't even been drafted yet, and I was beginning to feel like I had even more privilege than just being a high school basketball phenom. It was a good feeling though, none of that throw-your-head-back-in-the-sky fakeness. I was just proud that morning of what I was about to accomplish, and Jalen was happy for me too.

"So when you going to announce?" Jalen wanted to know.

"Don't know. I have to tell Mom, Tori, and Coach first."

"And your pops, *L*. You can't forget about your pops."

"Look, man, I'm not telling that—"

"Nope. Not even going to let you say it. He needs to hear it before he hears it off the street. It's only right."

I looked down at Jalen and knew his Ja Rule-looking, skee-ball, black-smoke-complexion ass was right. I guess it was just the principle of the whole thing. My pops had walked out on my mother without a word of explanation, or a dollar to pay any rent or buy milk, so taking the high road wasn't going to be easy, even though he had tried to reach out in his own kind of way for the past couple of years.

He wanted to be my father, but I wanted to keep him at bay. I wasn't feeling that Boyz N the Hood-start-living-and-learning-from-your-father move. He just never seemed to get it, and at that point in my life, I didn't want to hear anything he had to say. I admit, he spent the time to send sneakers before my games, but I never wore a pair. He sent money, and not once had I ever spent a dime of it. Jalen thought I was insane not letting him in, probably because his father was on lock and he wanted that father-son thing bad.

But I had my reasons and wanted my so-called father to realize he wasn't buttering up no punk. I had gotten along without him up to this point, and I didn't want him in my life after he let my mother struggle for years without a word.

Then he had the nerve to just pop up with gifts. Material things never make it right. He could have been a man and sat down and explained to me why he disappeared on us. Tell me why he left her when the rent was due while I was breast-feeding.

I wondered sometimes if he even knew we lived on the streets for days until the apartment in the projects opened up. To this day it turns my stomach that it almost came to a point where my mom thought about placing me in Child Services when she didn't know if she had what it took to raise a son all by herself.

With all of my issues I had with my father now in the past but not forgotten, something was telling me Jalen was right. I decided I would tell him I was planning to play overseas. Maybe even get some pleasure out of seeing the look on his face when he thinks of what became of what he left behind. I knew my intentions weren't right at that moment, but it was how I was thinking, and that's real.

"Okay, man. Damn! I'll tell him."

"You just not saying that, right? You know how gossip runs around this place. A minute after you announce, it's going to spread like a good bag of weed."

"I said I would. You just make sure you keep your mouth closed until I get a chance to tell everybody."

Jalen didn't answer back. His eyes were in the parking lot of the school. He was looking at Tori sitting on the hood of his car, talking through the window of someone driving a tricked-out black Escalade in gold trim. "Who she talking to?" he wondered out loud.

Before we even had a chance to walk over, the car door opened, and out came legs wearing silk suit pants and shined up leather kicks, topped off with a white button-down shirt and a nice silk tie.

"Aww, man, it's Toy," Jalen whispered with disgust.

As we got closer to his car, Toy's smile was getting wider by the second. We stopped when we reached his car, and Jalen took a walk around his ride to inspect his rims and wheels.

"Well, if it isn't my man, Langston," Toy said, trying to game me.

"I already told you, I'm not your man."

After Jalen finished bum-rushing Toy's wheels, he stood next to me.

Toy asked, "You like that, J?"

Jalen shrugged his shoulders. "It's a'ight."

Toy laughed him off. "Well, when you get one, park it next to mine. Then we can exchange some secrets, okay."

Jalen looked over at his own car when he noticed Toy looking at it. "Whatever, man."

"So what are you doing here?" I stepped over to Tori and put my arm around her. She kissed me on my cheek, and we all waited for Toy's answer.

He put a stick of gum in his mouth. "You have to ask?"

Toy had been chasing me around for the last six months with all his agent and representation talk for me to sign with him and his new sports rep company. Toy was okay, if you liked the thugs who were involved in everything in the streets and had a little book smarts. If his name didn't ring out with so much negativity in the streets, I might have listened to what he had to say. Toy was one of the superstar ballers that came out of The Vil and probably the only one who was at least smart enough to get his college degree. He now called himself a sports agent, among other things, so I was staying clear of him because if I'd signed with an agent, I would've lost my eligibility to go to college if the draft fell through.

"I already told you, Toy, no way I'm signing."

"Look, is it okay if I talk to you like a man in front of your people?"

I looked around at Tori then Jalen. "You can say what you feel."

Jalen said, "Don't mean a thing anyway. *L* ain't doing business with you, Toy."

Toy looked at all of us before he spoke. His eyes stayed on Jalen a bit longer though. "See, that's what I'm talking about. You taking advice from your boy, and he ain't never stepped foot out of Columbus."

"I've been plenty of places," Jalen shot back.

"Yeah, sure. Listen to me, Langston. You're ready. You're a six-seven shooting guard with quick feet and defensive skills. Every trade magazine in the country has you listed a first-round lottery pick, and they know you can't even play until you do one in college. You have the kind of face that people gravitate to, and the game to match, and for a high school kid you're pretty bright."

Tori looked up at me and smiled.

"And so?"

"You don't know? It means you're marketable. You have what it takes to make millions of dollars. If you think I'm putting pressure on you, wait for a few more weeks when those white boys from all those big corporate-controlled agencies come down here and entice your young ass with any and everything to get you to sign so they can get some of you."

"Well, you want some too, don't you?" Jalen asked.

Toy smiled at him. "I do. No doubt. But what I want is to build a dynasty with *L*. I want to unite and do this thing right. If you didn't know, everyone in the hood is looking at you to see what you're going to do. And they constantly have their eyes on me, and if we could just build something, build a brand together, it would let everyone in the hood know they can do it on both ends, on the court and in the business room. Besides, if you didn't know, there hasn't been a player who averaged thirty-five points, sixteen rebounds, and fourteen assists since . . . me."

Toy smiled and flirted with Tori with his eyes, like she would even be interested in his old ass.

Toy was a beast on the court in his day. Even though he came up when I was still trying to decide if I wanted to swing on the monkey bars or play in the sand, his name still swirled around the courts like one of those headless horsemen. He definitely had legacy in The Vil.

"Look, man, I'm just not ready to make a commitment like that. I haven't even graduated yet."

"Well, okay, okay." Toy added, "Maybe we should talk about it more, over your place with your mother. It would be good to break bread where I grew up."

"Naah. No, thanks," I told him.

"You know the league already put restrictions on entry, L, but I have some very creative ways to get you paid."

"No, thanks, Toy."

"Look, nobody turns down stacks of millions of dollars. It just doesn't make sense. If you're thinking about going to school, I understand that too. But, hell, you can buy a college after you get paid. I went to school, and this you should know. If they were slinging around multimillion-dollar contracts when I was coming out of high school, the only question I would have asked them fools is the line to sign on." Toy looked in his hand, hit a button on his key chain, and his car started up, the music pounding. Then he smiled and looked at Jalen. "Tight, ain't it?"

Chapter Three

Hit, or What?

I went to see Coach Pierce after lunch. Before he could give me another stack of college letters or tell me which recruiter promised what, I let him know I was going pro. Coach stared at me for a long while without words. He looked sad, like he was losing a son who was going to Iraq or something. I admit, Coach was always there for me. I'd known him since the seventh grade, ever since he began to make a habit out of coming to see my home games in middle school and pulling me to the side to give me a few pointers on my game. He was actually my first real experience being recruited. He would call and come over my house to make sure I would be enrolling at East High instead of the other schools that wanted me to hop on the bus and ride up to two hours just so their school could shine on the hardwood floor.

When I left Coach's office, I was cool. I felt like I had made the right decision, because he didn't try to turn me away from what I decided. Coach Pierce let me know that he was going to get a press conference set up, and told me not to worry about a thing except being there and announcing my intentions.

After talking to Coach, I skipped eighth and ninth periods. I told Jalen and Tori I was going to walk home to clear my head before I told my mom my decision because I didn't know how she was going to react. Probably be pissed. Since the college letters began to come in the ninth grade, she always wanted me to go to UCLA. She was always so serious about school.

There were times when she would stand over me at the kitchen table and make sure I did my homework. When I got impatient because I couldn't grasp the concept of a trig problem, I remember telling her I was wasting my time with all the books because no one was going to hire me when I got out of school anyway because I was black. It was the last time she smacked me, and just thinking about it always puts me in the right frame of mind. She told me that I was never to let something like the color of my skin hold me back, especially on my own accord. But in the same spirit my mother stressed the importance of how difficult it was going to be for me in the world. She didn't sugarcoat it, and that's exactly why I chose to go overseas and play then to the NBA afterwards.

It wasn't like I made my decision overnight. I had been thinking about it for months before Barcelona's call. I put things down on paper and made my decision. I thought about if I went to college how we would still more than likely have to struggle and continue to live in the projects. There was no doubt I would have to ask my mother for support to live on campus, when we were barely making it in The Vil.

It had always been hard for me to comprehend why people thought athletes had it made when they go to college. I'd heard stories from the athletes themselves where they can't take money from people, or aren't allowed to make money off jerseys that the school sells with the athlete's name on the back. I have never been with someone making money off someone else's blood, sweat, and tears. After all, the only thing the athlete receives out of all the money colleges make is a college diploma that he doesn't spend as much time obtaining as other students who aren't involved in sports, because there is so much team practice involved.

I carried good grades in school, but my mother made sure that I studied. If I wasn't home at a certain time, Coach knew my mother would come out to the school and pull me out of practice and jump all over him. But in college, it's your job, and your mama can't help you then. I have never understood how football and basketball players in college did their schoolwork, with all the tournaments they have, combined with practice. Maybe that's why the graduation rate is so low among the athletes because they go to school in the first place to have the opportunity to go pro.

I used all five of my visits that were allowed for recruits to choose a program. Out of all the ballplayers I met, not one thought he wasn't going to make it to the league, including the guys who didn't get any time. I didn't like that aspect of college, and that's why I decided to play overseas first.

My walk and thoughts about the situation were getting me hyped up to tell my mom of my decision because I knew she would go there. I was a few blocks from home when I heard someone calling out to me.

"Hey, big baller!"

I turned around to see who it was.

"Don't be acting like you don't know my voice, boy."

Then I felt a tug on my shirt.

"Girl, don't be sneaking up on me like that. What's up?"

Katrina said, "Where you goin'?"

"On my way home."

"Good. Me too. I don't feel like doing Mr. Dean's class today. Plus, it's my last class of the day. I will get with him later."

"You better take your butt back to class, Katrina. You know Dean don't play that."

"Whatever. Why you not up in there then?"

"'Cause I have a scout I need to talk to."

"Get out of here with that, Langston. You be straight milkin' this all-American status, don't you?"

"Somebody's got to do it."

"Well, later for Dean and his acronym-slinging ass." Katrina looked behind us then squeezed my butt.

"Oh, you just going to touch me like that all out in the open?"

"I missed you, *L.* I mean, it ain't like you have been touch-ing on me. Where have you been anyway?"

"Been handling mine, working out, whatnot."

"Yo' ass been hanging with Tori. That's what you been doing. I heard y'all was at the mall the other day. You don't have to lie."

I looked down at Katrina's smiling face and couldn't help but smile back at her. Out of all the girls who I knew had a crush on me, she was the most aggressive.

"Yeah, I been hanging with her too. Now what?"

"Oh, so now it's 'now what'? Boy, please."

Katrina rolled her eyes at me then walked in front of me like she didn't want to be bothered. She had to know I was peeping how her Apple Bottoms jeans were fitting her. As she walked, she snatched off her button-down sweater and let her matching, tight-fitting tee that stopped just above her tattoo along the small of her back shine for all to see.

"A'ight, a'ight. Hold up, Katrina," I called out.

She kept walking, but now her walk was harder than any contestant on *America's Next Top Model.*

"Girl, are you going to walk with me or what?"

She yelled back as she slowed down, "You gonna act like you know somebody or what?"

"Okay, okay."

"You sure, mister basketball star?"

"Look, I said okay." I jogged up to her. "Got a million games, don't you?"

"No, you're the one with the game, Langston."

"Oh, I got game?"

Katrina put her hand on her hip. She knew I was look-ing her up and down. She knew how to work her look and make sure all eyes were on her when she wanted to get your atten-tion. Katrina was about five feet nine inches, 145 pounds. with a smoking body that made even the girls look at her on a daily basis. She kept her hair in a ponytail and loved to rock low-cut jeans and short tees. I don't know if it was just me, but she reminded me of Rema Ma.

Katrina once wore a dress in the spring time, and when the administrator saw her in the dress and the lining of her thong, he stared at her for about five minutes. When his eyes were full, he told her to go home and change because she was way too much of a distraction.

"You mean like how you played me last week and told me you were coming over and never did? I always told you that I have to make sure people are out the house when you come over, and I did what I had to do. Then yo' ass don't even show up."

Katrina was right. I did promise. But I couldn't even remember the reason I didn't go over to see her, so I just stood looking at her with nothing to say.

"And don't tell me it was because some scout was at your house."

"Come to think of it, there were three there last week. North Carolina, Kansas came through then O State." I tried to touch her arm.

She moved away. "Whateva. You be playing games, man."

"I'm not playing any games. Don't you want me to get into school?"

"Of course, I want your black ass to get out of here. But they've been after you forever. What you need to do is be a man and make up your mind and handle this business right here when you get a chance."

"You know it's not that easy, Katrina. I need to make the right choice. I have to make this money."

"Yeah, yeah."

"But getting back to you . . . I just might handle some business sooner than you think."

Katrina smiled. "So what you doin' now?"

I pointed down the street. "I'm going home."

"Well, you need to be coming over my place. Nobody home. I bet you don't even know how long it's been since we been together."

"Katrina, I don't know."

"If you weren't all up in Tori, you would know. It was the week of your state championship game. That's a long time, Langston."

"Long time?"

"Yeah, it is. Didn't you like it? I mean, you must have. You got right up, left my house then went down to the Center and scored forty-five points."

"So, you think you had something to do with that?"

"I know I did. I mean, I know Tori didn't . . . 'cause she still a virgin. Oops!"

Everybody knew about Tori. Some even hated her for it because it set her up as a princess in The Vil. That was the price for living there. You learn early on that everyone in The Vil knows everybody, and it's tell one, tell all.

I didn't have to hide from Tori the fact that I messed around with Katrina. She knew, and was with it. I wasn't too young to know that putting it in Tori's face wasn't cool, so I respected her and did whatever I had to do with Katrina on the hush. At least my mouth was closed.

Tori was cool, and that's what I liked most about her. She was so real. Real enough to know that things happen. We had talked about it many times, and she left what I did with Katrina up to me. She wanted it to be my choice and didn't really think it was fair for her to ask me to wait, even though she had decided to. Tori's five sisters were the reason for her actions. Each one ended up pregnant before getting out of high school, and she didn't want to join the club.

Katrina and Tori were as different as night and day. Even though Tori lived in the hood, she had ideas and was working the best out of what little options she had to make it out. But Katrina was a hood rat who ran game to get hers at all cost and never talked about doing much with her life, except living in some house somewhere on the East side.

By the time we were back in The Vil, Katrina had talked me into going over in her unit and giving her what she wanted. It wasn't all on her, because I wanted it too.

Chapter Four
Bills, Bills, Bills

When I got home around six, my mother was doing her nails. There was no room left on the couch because she was all spread out, doing her toes and whatnot, so I plopped down on the floor across from her after I kissed her on the cheek.

" 'Sup, Ma?"

"Hey," she said. She was watching a movie too while polishing. She finally looked over at me before I could see what she was watching. "So where you been?"

"Huh?"

"You heard me. Where have you been?"

I didn't know if she had already got a call from someone who saw me creeping with Katrina or what. "School, talking to Coach."

She gave me a long stare down like she didn't believe me. "What?"

"My phone has been ringing off the hook since three o'clock. Did you tell Tori you were going to meet her someplace?"

"What?"

"Tori's been calling you. How many times I have to tell you, Langston? You tell a woman you're going to do something then, boy, you make sure you do it."

I couldn't help but snicker at my mom.

"Don't you dare laugh. You know I taught you better. I hate to think you're trying to be a player up in here like the rest of these no-good men."

One thing's for sure, a mother that's been wronged by a

man definitely will let a young black man know the deal without biting her tongue. My mother did all the time.

"I just told Tori I would meet her at the library. I'll go over there in a minute."

"Too late."

"What you mean by that?"

"She's coming over here."

"Why?"

"'Cause I told her to."

"For what?"

"So I could see her, talk to her."

"Ma, you just like Tori 'cause she's a virgin."

"What's wrong with that? That means she respects herself. Plus, she looks like me."

"What?"

"You know how fine your mama is, and you went out and found a girl that looks just like her. I ain't mad at you."

"You are buggin'!"

"Our eyes are brown, we keep our hair fierce. Everybody at the games say we look alike, so get over it."

I glanced at my mom and tried to see what she was talking about. I didn't see it, except for maybe a little around the eyes, and skin color. But all I know is, growing up, the men around The Vil would try to get in good with me, hoping I would take a liking to them so they could step to her, always calling out, 'Golden Brown,' to her.

When I was around nine or ten, that's when I started to walk behind my mother if we were outside, so those fools on the block couldn't look at her butt. She didn't figure out what I was doing until I was about fourteen. She told me there was no reason to hide her from those fools' eyes because they didn't have a chance at getting with her because she already had a man, and that man was me.

"I see you lookin' at me, Langston. Now admit it—Don't I look like your girl?"

"Okay, okay, you look like Tori."

"No, no, she looks like me, and don't you forget it."

"Okay."

"And she's the one you should be concentrating on, instead of some of these chickens running around here doing everything and everybody."

"What you mean by that?"

"You know what I mean. Don't try to play your mama."

My mother had never been afraid to get all up in my business. She always told me my business was hers until the day she died. It was the price I paid for having a mother in her thirties with a whole lot of street wisdom behind her. She knew things, lived things, and was able to relate them to me, which a lot of times kept me from taking the wrong step. It was as though my mom knew what I was thinking before I even thought it because she knew what our surroundings were about and the type of trouble I could get into.

For the longest my mother tried to teach me about the police and what I should do if I was ever taken downtown or stopped. She would stand me up hours at a time and cover different situations that could happen to me with them, saying, "Be courteous. Stay calm. Never admit to anything. Keep your hands where they can see them. Never reach in your pocket. Only tell them your name. They have to ask to search you or the car. Tell them to call your mother, and never sign anything."

Sometimes she would get angry with me because I couldn't understand why the police would stop me if I had done nothing wrong. She would tell me, "It would take a man to make you really understand, but I'm all you have. So you need to listen to me and take my advice."

"So how long ago you talk to Tori?"

"'Bout thirty minutes ago. She should be here any minute."

"Well, I'm goin' to shower."

"Why?"

"'Cause I want to have on something fresh when she gets here." I looked down next to my mother and noticed the bills she had thrown on the table. "Hey, Ma, wouldn't it be nice to have someone take care of all those bills for you?"

"Don't worry, baby. We'll get through it, just like we always do."

"I bet a first-round draft pick could handle those for you and then some."

It took a few seconds for my mother to really hear what I said to her. Then she looked up at me while blowing her nails. "What did you just say?"

"I'm going pro overseas. I'm putting my name in the draft. Barcelona called last night and said they were taking me number one."

I was preparing myself to go over everything with her that I'd thought about on my walk home. I waited for her questions, even an explosion of anger, but it never came. Mom was motionless, her eyes on me like I remembered them to be when I was a baby wearing Pull-Ups and holding my sippy cup. Then a tear rolled down her face.

"You sure this is what you want to do, baby?"

"Ma, you know it's what I always wanted to do. I am thinking, one, no more than two years with Barcelona then the NBA. It's the only way to bypass these rules and make money so I can take care of things for you."

She didn't say another word. She stood up, wiped her tears with the palms of her hands, and gave me the longest hug ever. "I am so proud of you, Langston, so proud."

Chapter Five
Need to Know

By the time I was out of the shower, Tori had already come over and was sitting next to my mother. She was looking at the nail polish scattered around and listening to her blow up the fact that I decided I to go pro.

"Ma, you told?"

"You didn't tell me not to." She pushed with a big smile.

"It's all right, *L*. What mother could hold back that her baby was going pro?" Tori was excited and reminding me at the same time that she had my mother in the palm of her hand.

"Not one I know," my mother said. "I'm calling your so-called father next."

"No, no. Let me do it," I told her.

She looked up at me. "You sure? You haven't called him since you were ten."

"Yeah, I'm sure."

She threw the phone over to me.

I sat it down. "Uh-uh. I'm going over to his house to tell him."

My mother and Tori had blank expressions. They knew how I felt about my father. Thank God, I didn't have to explain my decision, because there was a knock on the door.

"What er'body up in here so happy about?" Jalen asked as soon as he walked in.

"My baby goin' pro!"

Jalen played it off on the joke tip. "You just now finding that out, Reecy?"

"You already know?"

"What don't I know? is the question," Jalen boasted.

Mom told him, "Boy, if you don't shut up, talking all that mess . . ."

"So, *L*, what's up, baby? If you haven't realized, you gotta lot of shit"—Jalen put his hands over his mouth then looked at my moms. "Sorry 'bout that, but a brother like me is excited too."

"Boy, go 'head and say what you sayin'," she told him. "Maybe it's something good."

Jalen put his hands in his pockets. "L, you got things to do, man, and look, I'm the man who going to help you out. I went over to the library, you know, and ol'girl who was, like, promising me last week at the party that she was gonna—"

"Jalen, I really don't want to hear about your skanks," Mom said.

"I don't either. You should see them, Reecy."

My mother turned to Tori. "They nasty?"

"Mmm-hmm. If you only knew."

"Oh, I'll pass." Then my mother turned and gave Tori some dap.

"Y'all really need to stop hating. I gets mine."

"Yeah, you get it, all right," Tori told him.

My mother started to laugh. "But the question is, can you get rid of it?"

This time Tori gave my mom some dap.

"Are y'all putting a new comedy show together or something?" Jalen said. "'Cause if you are, let me be the first to let you know your material is wack."

"Jalen, finish, man," I told him.

"So, what you want to hear about? The girl at the library or this drama right here?"

My mother nodded toward Jalen. "Okay, tell us about what you have in your hand, boy."

"First, I ran off some copies of this article where LeBron James is weighing his options about playing overseas and getting like fifty million a year. He thinking about going over there, play a few years, then back in the NBA. Not only that, Earl Boykin ain't thinking about it. He just signed for like four million for just one year. And Josh Childress he got thirty big dogs for three years. Now, *L*, as I see it, with you going over there, they going to break you off no less than *fit-teen* mil a year, baby, so you might as well get that passport ready."

"*L*, are they payin' like that overseas?"

Jalen butted in before I could answer. "Yeah, they paying like that, with your lucky self. That's if *L* decide to keep you around."

"Shut up, Jalen!" I told him.

My mother put her arm around Tori.

"Next I have some of those sports agencies that handle all the top stars, which we know you going to be. We got to get cracking and start calling them to let them know a brother like you goin' to be available and you want to play one or two seasons overseas then we in the NBA. You heard what Toy said—They are goin' to be after you. So it's better if you contact the best first, and weed out all the rest."

"Toy?" My mother blurted out.

"Don't worry, Reecy. Toy is not an issue in this circle."

"Look, boy, I already let you slip up once in my house. Call me by my first name again and bet you don't get a fat lip."

"Would y'all just hold up." I looked at Tori as she laughed at Jalen and all of his craziness. "Look, all I want to do is go tell the man who got my mother pregnant with me what I plan to do. Then we can sit down and talk about all this. Right here on the couch, okay."

Jalen was thinking and mumbled to himself, "The man that got your mother pregnant . . . that's yo' daddy, right?"

"Somebody smack him," my mother pleaded. "Just smack all the taste out of his mouth."

Chapter Six

You Don't Know Me

Jalen had a few beers on ice in the car. When I found out, I made him drink them and told Tori to drive over to my father's. I wasn't getting caught up in the car, with him drinking and driving, when I was about to announce my entrance overseas.

It didn't take long to get over to where he stayed. He was on the East side but closer to downtown, in a neighborhood off Bryson Road. It was rough over there too. Lots of fools always beefing about some nonsense, and prostitution from time to time. I always knew where he stayed. One time, my mother had a job interview in Cincinnati, and he watched me. I'd spent the day with him and hated every minute of it, and hadn't been back since.

I didn't want to deal with what I knew more than likely was going on inside, so I had Tori by the hand for support. I also gave Jalen, like, three mints and some gum, to cover that beer up before knocking on the door.

He answered.

Damn! I felt myself squeeze Tori's hand extra tight.

"Hi, Langston." He then looked at Tori and Jalen. "C'mon in, you guys. Your father will be down in a minute."

I couldn't believe the man who got my mother pregnant was letting his boyfriend answer the door. It almost made me lose my mind. I looked over at Jalen, who was about to laugh about the way this guy was walking as he went to get the man that made me.

My mother's sperm donor's friend, partner, or whatever you want to call him went by the name of Kenny. From what I knew about him, he was a lawyer. I really didn't care to know anymore about him because he turned my stomach. I was just happy he answered the door and went into another room so I didn't have to look at him. To me he was disgusting, and I didn't like the way he tried to play me like he really knew me, because it wasn't like that at all.

After a long two minutes, the man that walked out on me and my mother finally walked into the living room, where we were sitting. On the real, his place was nice. He had hardwood floors running all the way through it and had it dressed up tight with lots of colorful art. It was just what was happening inside of the house that made it ugly to me because of the way he left me to be in it. If he wasn't living up in there with the man, I could probably work through some of what he did to my mom, but not this way. There was no way I could.

He smiled when he walked in and stood over me with his arms outstretched to give me a hug. I kind of smiled at him, but a hug, I was not giving.

When he realized that a handshake was the only thing he was getting from me, he sat across from all of us in a chair. "You look good, Langston. What are you now, six-six, two twenty?"

"Naah. Six-seven and a half, two forty."

"I don't know where you got all this height and weight from."

"He's blessed!" Jalen shouted out then smiled.

"Jalen, how are you doing? How's your father?"

"I'm good, but he's back in jail."

"I see. Did you bring me something to drink?"

Jalen was surprised.

"I saw you over at the drive-thru on Livingston."

"Oh yeah. I was getting some soda and some Gatorade," he explained.

Then he nodded in Tori's direction. "So who do we have here?"

Tori smiled. She knew how I felt about my father, but she didn't have a grudge about it. She'd even tried once or twice to get me to open up to him, but I wasn't having it. "I'm Tori," she said.

I let him know as strong as I could. "*She's my girl.*"

He picked up on my tone then ran some quick questions by me.

"Okay, so what brings you over? Need anything? You're still graduating, right? You pick a school yet? I've been waiting to hear something in the news about it."

"Yeah, we all graduate in a few weeks. Just came by to give you some news though."

He looked at Tori hard. "You're not pregnant, are you?"

Tori moved her head back a bit then shook it no, with kind of a snarl on her face.

"No, she's not pregnant, man."

He looked at her then apologized.

"Look, I just came over to tell you that I'm not going to college. I'm going overseas to play ball for at least one year, maybe two, then to the NBA."

The forced smile he was trying to display to us quickly disappeared, and his voice dropped a bit. "Overseas?"

"That's right!" Jalen said. "*L* is going to set that league on fire. Then he coming back to the States and show what it is."

"So you're going to forgo your education to pursue some hoop dream?"

Tori held my hand extra tight.

"Yup. I got a call from the front office of Barcelona. They want to take me number one."

He was silent.

"What?"

"I don't think it's a good idea."

"Why not?"

"I don't know if you're ready. You'll be playing with grown men, Langston, in another country."

"I play with them all the time, and all the rims all over the world round and the backboards square."

"Not on this level. It's a whole different game."

"Yeah, I know that's why, as soon as graduation is over, I'm going over to start working out and get in the flow of things."

He paused and started thinking. He started to say something but turned his head and waited a few seconds. "So it sounds like this is pretty much a done deal? Nothing can be said to hold you back?"

"I made up my mind last night, told Barcelona I would love to play for them. Just told mom, and you were next on the list."

"And how does your mother feel about it?"

"She's cool with it. Told me the sky is the limit."

Kenny walked in from the hallway, where he was all up in our business. He peeked out and said with his feminine voice, "Of course, she is."

I stood up. "What you say about my mother?"

"I just—"

At the moment his voice was giving me the creeps, and I didn't want to hear it anymore so I cut him off and just snapped. "You don't know me, you understand? And you don't know my mother. So you don't have a right to say a damn thing about what the hell goes on in my life."

Kenny's boyfriend told me to calm down.

"Calm down? Forget that! First of all, I didn't come over here to ask your permission, man. I came over here to let you know my plans for my life. My life . . . the life that you thought wasn't good enough to stick around for because you felt you wanted to lay up in here with this punk."

Now he was on his feet too. I was waiting for him to swing, so I could knock his ass out.

"You better watch your mouth, boy."

I inched closer to him and felt him move back an inch or two. "Or what? What you going to do to me?" I turned around grabbed Tori by the hand and lifted her up out of her seat. "I'm out of here."

Chapter Seven

Up in Here

Jalen wasn't bumping his system on the way home. All we could hear was the tires rolling on the pavement. With a cigarette dangling from his lip and one eye squinted to keep the smoke out, Jalen tried to keep his other eye on the road. Tori was sitting in between us in the front seat. I could tell she was trying not to cry. She always hated drama. Most of the way home I just looked out the window. I couldn't wait to get away. The man that made me was just that. I decided it was probably the last conversation I would ever have with him.

When Jalen pulled up in front of my unit, I couldn't believe Toy's car was parked in front. We stepped inside, and there was Slick Willy sitting on our couch, talking to my mom.

"What you doin' here, man?"

Toy looked at my mother with a fake smile then back at me. "Congrats on your decision to turn pro. I see you finally decided to take my advice."

"Man, what are you talking about?"

He looked at my mother again, trying to draw her in. "I was just telling Reecy how I've been talking to you on and off about this very subject."

Mom was sharp and to the point. "And I was just telling you, Toy, my son has told me all about you and your advice."

Toy looked at me then back at my mother. "Oh, is that right?"

I nodded at him.

"Well, good. Then you know what kind of a future I think *L* has."

"Yes, I know he has a very bright future, Toy. He's worked very hard for everything he's gotten so far."

"And that's why I decided to come here, Reecy . . . when I heard he took my advice."

"You didn't have a thing to do with it, Toy," Jalen told him. "Stop trying to get in, man."

Toy tried to brush Jalen off. "Like I said, when I heard he was going pro, I wanted to come over and let your mother know everything she will be up against."

I didn't notice until then, but our phone had been ringing off the hook since I walked back in the house.

"Mom, aren't you going to get that?"

"Baby, that phone has been ringing like that since you left."

"Why?"

"I don't know. I just called a few people, told them about your decision, and ever since, it won't stop ringing."

"Reecy, you want me to get it?" Tori asked.

"Reecy?" Jalen looked at my mom, waiting for her to blow, but it never happened.

"Tori, take a message for me, baby, okay."

Tori looked at Jalen and smiled then walked into the kitchen to get the phone.

"Like I was saying, I think it's time you sit down and start to look at things from a business perspective."

My mother asked, "Like what, Toy?"

"And what makes you think I wanna sit down with you?" I asked him next.

"That's what I'm saying," Jalen added.

"Because you should, young brother. I'm from the hood. I understand your needs, and I'm qualified to tell you the odds and ends of marketing on the pro level that will enable you to maximize your profits."

"Oh, the money. Now we're getting down to it," I told him

"But you're not saying anything, Toy. What do you want from my son?"

"Reecy, you know I only want the best for him and, of course, you. I want to represent L. I want to be his agent and get him the most money from the team that drafts him, and endorsements that are sure to follow. Look at the boy! Tell me he couldn't sell anything you put in his hands."

Tori walked back in and gave my mother a written message from the phone call. Then the phone started to ring again, and she went back to it.

My mother asked him, "So when do you want us to sign?"

"The sooner the better. It's time to get on the phone now."

"And you care about my son?"

"Look, I still remember him getting in the way on the courts when I was trying to ball," Toy told her.

"Well, if you cared anything about him, Toy, you wouldn't be here trying to get him to sign. You know just as well as I do, if something happens where he doesn't get picked up in the draft or gets hurt beforehand and signs with an agent he won't be able to go to college."

Toy laughed from embarrassment after the words he was searching for couldn't come out. "But, look, he's a sure thing."

Moms told him, "Good-bye, Toy."

"But—"

I opened the door for him. "You heard her. Later." I sat down on the couch, already tired of the drama.

Tori came back in with another message, and Jalen sat on the floor next to the front door.

My mother started to read the messages.

"Can you believe people asking me for a loan? They want to know, when you get your contract, can I loan them some money. I tell you, people are a trip." She looked over at me. "So what did your father have to say?"

"Forget him. I ain't trying to talk about what he saying. I don't even know why I went over there in the first place."

"That was my fault, man. I thought he might want to hear about it, you know. I guess I was thinking about my pops and how he hates to hear what I'm doing out in these streets by somebody other than me," Jalen said.

"Tell me what he said," Mom pushed.

"It wasn't really his father," Tori let her know. "It was Kenny."

"Kenny?"

I sank farther down on the couch. I knew it was coming.

"Oh, is that the name of his friend?"

"I guess," I told her.

"What did *he* have to say?"

"Just forget about it, okay."

"Boy, you want your last beat-down before you go overseas to be in front of your friends? Tell me what he said."

"Mom, whatever. He just said something like, of course you want me to go pro."

"Wait a minute. Do I even know him?"

"Naah, you don't know him."

"And he put my name in his mouth?"

"Sure did. Like y'all used to dance at the club or something," Jalen said.

"And he don't know me?" My mother grabbed her bag and went to the door. "Look, I will be back, okay."

"Mom, where are you going?"

"Where do you think I'm going? I raised you all by myself for eighteen years, and ain't nobody going to say a word about anything that's concerning what you want to do with your life, or what I think about it."

I didn't get to say another word because, after she told Jalen to get his ass from in front of the door, she was gone.

Tori turned the television, equipped with bootleg cable,

to MTV then sat down on the couch next to me. Jalen sat back on the floor in front of the TV.

"So, what's up now, *L*?" Jalen asked.

"I ain't trippin', believe that."

"Don't worry about all that drama, *L*. You already made up your mind. You just have to do you." Tori started rubbing my hand.

I got up from the couch. "I'm not worrying about it. I'm trying to celebrate." I went back to the hall closet and came out with one of my shoeboxes and sat back down next to Tori. "We're goin' to have a party." I opened the box and showed them all the money inside.

Jalen jumped up. "See, that's what I'm talking about!"

"Dang, baby! Where you get all that from?"

"From him. He started sending me money like two years ago like water, but I never wanted it. I just started putting it in here."

"It has to be at least six gees, man." Jalen put his hand in the box, pulled some out, and made it rain.

"Maybe. I never counted it." I pulled some money out and gave to Tori. "Here, go get some gear for this party, okay. Get your nails and hair done if you want. And, Jalen, buy you some sneakers, man, and then set this party up." I took another handful of money and put it on the table. "That's for Reecy. So, y'all ready to party or what?"

Chapter Eight
Ride with Me

Jalen was ghost once he got a pocket full of money. He walked out the door claiming he was going to get the tightest shoes on the racks and put together a party like The Vil had never seen. Tori was just happy he was gone because she had been waiting to talk to me alone all day.

"So what you think your mother doing?" She smiled.

"Oh, you know what she's doing. She's over there ripping up the place."

"So you really don't like your father, *L?*"

"C'mon, girl, I barely know him, and what I do know about him, I don't like."

"At least you know he's alive. I don't even know the name of my father."

"You ever asked about him?"

"A few times, but I never get an answer."

"What you mean by that?"

"When I ask about him, my mother never gives me an answer. I have caught her in so many lies about who he is and what he does, I just got frustrated and stopped asking. She makes me think that she doesn't even know who he is . . . old ho." Tori laughed a bit.

"So all you know is that he's black?"

"That's it."

"Well, he must have tore your mother up when he made you."

"Boy, what are you talking about?"

"I'm just saying . . . 'cause you so fine. He must have bust a special one."

Tori hit me on the leg and showed me that smile again. Then she took my arm, wrapped it around her shoulders, and sat underneath me.

"You know, *L*, it's a trip because I sit around and listen to my grandmother always talk about how things and families used to be, compared to the way things are around here. It's just so hard to believe some of the things she tells me that used to happen that people don't do these days."

I knew exactly what she was saying. "Like how people would whup somebody else's child when they saw them doing wrong?"

"Yup, and how families used to stick together, no matter what. I just can't believe that 'cause families around this joint fight every damn night until the police gotta come out and take somebody away."

"Ain't no love. Everybody out for self."

"Well, I'm not trying to live like that. If I tell a man that I'm going to be with him, then that's what the hell I'm goin' to do forever, so my kids can see the love."

"So who are you talking about?"

"What you mean?"

"The man you going to be with?"

"I'm just saying."

"What if it was me? How you know it won't be me?"

"Maybe. I mean, if you goin' to be him, then I would put my word on it that it would be forever and always straight love, boy."

"Umm, I likes that. Maybe we should get married."

"Boy, shut up!"

"I'm serious."

"No, you're not. How you goin' to marry me anyway?"

"What you mean, how?"

"You're going to be leaving soon."

"So?"

"And you're going to be playing ball overseas."

"And?"

"Shut up, Langston. This ain't nothing to be playing around with."

"Who's playing? Look, why don't we get married? I mean, you love me, don't you?"

"Fo' sho."

"And you know how I feel about you?"

"I guess I do."

"What you mean by that?"

"Say it. Tell me you love me."

"Girl, you know I love you. And we need to get married because I'm going to need somebody I can trust to watch my back when I go pro. I mean, we practically have seen and talked to each other every day since sixth grade, right? I'm not leaving you here and not be able to continue to see you every day."

Tori had this glazed look on her face and then smiled. "Yeah."

"Well, let's get married. I won't be right out there any other way."

"Are you sure?"

"C'mon, girl, ride with me."

Chapter Nine

If You Must

On Saturday morning I chilled in the bed until noon watching *SportsCenter* and the story that ran hour after hour confirming that I was going to go overseas to play ball. I didn't know who broke the story, but I did like hearing the sound of my name and seeing some highlights of some of my games over and over again.

I was so hyped over the news, I went outside in the hot sun and ran more than six miles on one of my routes through The Vil, up, down, and through the units, like I had done so many times before. This time, though, I was taking the atmosphere in and loving every second of where I grew up, instead of keeping my head straight down at the ground, blocking out the sights and sounds of people who had been there for years and probably their families who would be there for years to come.

After my run, I used my key to the gym at school that Coach gave to me and was inside working hard, still remembering the sound of my name on national television.

I yelled over to Jalen. "How many is that?" I knew I was close to a hundred and fifty jumpers. My plan was to do two hundred.

"Damn! Why you asking me? You're the one shooting," Jalen yelled. "What? I have to count and run after the rebounds too?" Jalen cussed at me then ran down to the other end of the court to get a ball that came off the back rim.

I couldn't help but laugh at the fool because he was sweating just as hard as I was. I took another shot. We were drilling with three balls. "C'mon, J, you're going to have to keep up.

I got to get my shot smooth like butter. You ever see how Jim Jackson used to keep his stroke on point when he got hot? I want my shot just like that, baby!"

Jalen threw a hard pass to me. "It's already butter. What done got into you, *L*?"

"They put my name on blast this morning on ESPN, baby!"

"For real?"

"On the real. You should be keeping up with that."

"How am I going to keep track with that and get this party together? Why didn't you call me?"

I caught another pass then shot. "Moms was on the phone talking about the drama over the man's house who got her pregnant with me."

"What happened?"

"You know she went over there and cussed his ass out."

"Man, yo' mama a trip. She don't let anybody mess with you, not even yo' daddy."

"That's my girl."

I asked Jalen how many more shots to go, and when he couldn't tell me, I decided to take twenty. "You gotta keep up with me, Jalen."

"Look, I have been doing this since you been able to touch the nets. Shut up and shoot."

I took my last shot then collapsed down to the floor. My eyes went up to all the banners that my team had received since my ninth grade year—three state championships and one state runner-up, which happened my sophomore year. And we would have won that game if I hadn't missed a jumper at the buzzer.

Jalen took a ball and sat down on it. "So you ready or what?"

"Yeah, I think so."

"Forget that, *L*! How you going to be thinking at a time like this? You either know, or you don't. We talking professional basketball."

I knew Jalen was right. And I liked the fact that he was able to be straight up with me and keep things real. He'd always been that way. "Yeah, man. I'm ready."

"Okay, then that's what I'm talking 'bout."

"What about you?"

Jalen said, "What you mean, me?"

"Are *you* ready?"

"Ready for what?"

"Ready for the pros."

"You're the one going to be playing, not me."

"But you're going with me, right?"

Jalen looked up from the floor and looked at me and smiled.

"You think I was going to let my boy stay here while I'm in another country all by my damn self?"

"Don't play, *L*. You know how I hate how you be playing so much."

"Word is bond, *B*. I want everybody who's been down since day one with me when I leave this place. I already thought about it. You're going to be my personal assistant and take care of my day-to-day business."

"What? Personal assistant?"

"Yeah."

"No way, man. It sounds gay."

"Shut the hell up, Jalen. I want you to stay close to me, man. You know how people get when someone plays pro sports. With everybody pulling and pushing to get next to the players, I'm going to need somebody I know who can handle all that for me, so I can concentrate on playing ball."

"You serious?"

"Why not? You've been doing it all this time."

"You sayin' I been your bitch, *L*?"

"No, you dumb-ass fool. You've been my friend."

"Well, I'll do it, but you ain't gonna be calling me your damn personal assistant though. That's not happening."

"All right. Think of something else to call it. But there's one catch. You have to go to school, man."

"School?"

"You heard me."

"For what?"

"So you can learn, man. Keep learning all about those endorsements and business deals you always throwing around. I want you to learn the business through whatever agency we hire to take care of everything, until you can handle it on your own. Plus, we only going overseas for a year or two. Then it's the NBA, baby!"

J's eyes bugged out his head. "Get outta here, L. You want me to run it?"

"That's right. Why shouldn't my boy get something out of this? Plus, I've been watching a few players in the league, and they keep their boys close. You don't throw your friends away."

"So, you want endorsements like that big-head li'l dude on those Sprite commercials?"

"I want those and then some."

"Ahh, man! I'm already getting enough loving from the ladies just by knowing you. Do you know how much that multiplies when we turn pro and I tell them I'm your handler?"

"Handler?"

"Yeah, I make it happen for you. That's what I do."

"A'ight, cool. Whatever you call it. Just bring your game every day."

"Don't worry, I always do. Ahh! Damn! Do you know how many females I'm goin' to get? It's going to be like I'm in the league too, but an executive or something."

"Are females the only thing you think about, J?"

"No, but I think about it more than you 'cause you don't have to think about them because they always around."

"Well, pretty soon that's going to be in the past."

"What you mean?"

I stood to my feet and started pounding the ball through my legs and around my back. "'Cause I'm getting married."

Jalen began to laugh. "You talking about going pro and getting married? You have lost your mind. If you didn't know, let me tell you something, mister all-American. Pro players play ball hard, and play the ladies even harder. Nothing but groupies all day long! I heard those players just give them a look like this and pucker their lips like this, and after the game, it's on!" Jalen had the nerve to pucker his lips and squint his eyes, pretending to nod at groupies.

"You look straight stupid, J."

"I'm telling you, L. It's like *Bam!* All you want for the taking. Then you go to the next city. Now who's going to give all that up?"

"I am. That's who."

"For who? For what?"

"For Tori . . . 'cause I love her."

"What you mean, in a couple of years or something?"

"No, as soon as we get overseas."

Jalen stood up and started dribbling then he took a shot and he didn't care if it went in or not. "So you're serious?"

"Man, I don't have time to play games. Tori's been down with me for the longest."

"And she a virgin," Jalen said with a silly-ass tone. "I mean, that's special enough, 'cause the last virgin was Mary, and Jesus hit that."

"You have problems—And that's not the only reason."

Jalen looked at me.

"Okay, it's a very good reason, but she's my girl, man. I have talked to her every day since forever, and she is part of me. Y'all like brother and sister anyway, so stop stressing."

"Yeah, you know she's my girl. You are dead serious about this, aren't you?"

I took a jumper, and it went straight down through the nets. "Yup, I'm doing it."

"A'ight, family . . . if you must."

Chapter Ten

Tired of Poverty

Jalen took a sip of a beer then lit up a joint. One thing about him, after a workout he was getting a cold brew and getting nice. He had a six and pulled a brew out of his brown bag and reached out to hand it to me.

When I reached out to take it, he pulled it back and said, "Nope. No drinking for you, and definitely none of this weed." Then he lit his joint.

"You act like I smoke every day," I told him.

"Once a year would be way too much." Jalen pulled out a big jug of Gatorade and handed me a protein bar. "Here, enjoy this."

We were standing outside in The Vil. It was the beginning of the month, and it was straight-up lovely because food was in the fridge, peeps were sporting new cuts and 'dos and, more than anything, had a few extra dollars that they could either save for an emergency or spend until the next batch of government checks rolled through.

"So you think you ever going to miss this place?" Jalen wanted to know.

I was looking at a drug deal going down, so Jalen had to wait a few before I answered him back. Watching deals on the street was nothing new, but ever since I was sitting on the street and almost got wet up when a crackhead thought he was going to straight jack a soldier for his keep, I had been paying more attention, so I could get out the way if need be. This time a soldier was leaning into a car, making sure the driver wasn't police, before he sent him down the street to cop. Then the car drove off, and he started looking around for his next customer.

I answered, "You mean, this day, this moment? Yeah, I'm going to miss this. Ain't nothing like hood love, you know."

"Yeah, the hood is rough, man, but the love is always genuine, you know."

"That's why, when I get my first check, I want to do something nice for The Vil."

"Like what? You already 'bout to throw the big party. I got it all set up. We going to have enough food to feed the entire Vil. The music going to be bumpin', but we drinking Kool-Aid though. You know you can't even buy enough liquor for these fools, so I'm not even going to try."

"Naah, man, not just a party. Something worth doing."

"Oh, don't get it twisted. They like to eat," Jalen said. "Yo' cousins and them will remember food and good music a long time, L."

"Are you high already, Jalen?"

Jalen puffed on his blunt. "Naah, not as high as I'm going to get."

"Man, I'm talking about something with some strength. Maybe build that rec center that was promised to the hood when we were young bucks by ol' boy who won the heavyweight championship."

"Oh yeah! I forgot all about that."

"A lot of people have. We're used to broken promises out here. We hear them all the time from everybody. You know how nice that would have been? You know how many people might have changed their life behind that promise?"

"What you mean, L?"

"I'm just saying, people see you do something and give back like that, and it more than likely will put on the brain that someone else can make it too."

"So that's what you want to do then?"

"Yeah, man, I do. Make sure you write that down as one of the first things we going to do when I get paid, even if I can only build a few courts around this piece to start showing I love the hood. I wanna do something."

We stood that night in our regular spot for hours chatting and thinking about our future. By the time I looked at my watch, it was close to one in the morning. I had just finished sending Tori a text message, and when I looked up Maddox and Granger were standing near the car, trying to bum the last two beers.

"Now you lames know you don't have a bit of sense," Jalen told them. "How you going to ask for the last two beers? What you think, *L*? Should I give it to them?"

I walked over and greeted the fools. We all used to hang like brothers, but things had changed. Granger and Maddox knew the streets was their calling, and they wasted no time getting out there and getting their hustle on.

I looked them both over because, to tell the truth, they looked a little nervous. "So what's up? What y'all been up to?"

"Aww, man, just chilling," Maddox said, a slight grin on his face.

"You know how we do, *L*, just making that money," Granger added.

"We ain't got to be worried about getting shot at tonight, do we?" Jalen wanted to know. "You pimps always in beef," he joked.

"Son, you in The Vil. What you think?" Maddox said. "Always be on the lookout, ya know."

Jalen gave them the beers and sat on the hood of his car right next to me.

"I hear you goin' pro overseas, *L*," Granger said, proud.

"Yeah, man, I gotta make that jump."

"Do that, do that!" Maddox punched like a rapper.

Maddox could ball too. Matter of fact, I would have

rated him in the top five who lived in The Vil as far as players went, right below Jalen. The only reason he didn't play ball for the school was because he didn't like Coach Pierce. Plus, he'd stopped going to school when we were sophomores to concentrate on being a dope runner.

Maddox looked me over. "So you tired of this poverty, L? Is that why you clearing out?"

"Yeah, man, it's time to get outta here."

"I don't blame you. I wish I would have kept playing some ball. Maybe I would be getting out this hole too." Maddox took his first taste of his beer. "Whew! This is ice-cold, baby."

"You know how we do it. Look, you like that, wait until tomorrow night. L having a party, and y'all better be there," Jalen told them. "Look for me in the car. I'ma have some more on ice for the good people."

"Going to have some freaks?" Granger yelled out.

"L goin' pro, man, so you know they all going to be here trying to get a piece."

Granger said, "Damn, L! How you going to handle all that lovin' from the ladies you going to be gettin'?"

"Man, I ain't going to have no time for that."

"No time for the ladies?" Maddox asked.

"Naah, man. I'm taking Tori with me, and we going to get married. She'll keep my mind off all that, so I can concentrate on the game."

"Man, you must be crazy," Maddox said. "No way I would tie myself down, with all that potential loving just ready to get tapped."

"Shut up!" Granger told him. "Look, you doin' the right thing, L. You got business to handle when you get up in there. Groupies don't do nothing but distract you anyway."

Except for the street soldiers slinging on the street, The Vil had become quiet. We weren't ready to go crash, and Maddox knew about a house party that didn't even start until one in the morning, so we went to check it out.

When we knocked on the door, a girl named Leo who had been trying to peep game answered, and her eyes were wide when she saw me standing there with my boys. Leo was thick, borderline fat, but she was still cute inside and out.

She was smiling and had her hand on her hip. "Y'all trying to get up in here, Langston?"

"Girl, what the heck you think?" Granger blasted while he was standing behind me. "Wit' your big ass."

I turned around and pushed him. "Don't worry about him. Yeah, we trying to party with y'all tonight."

"You going to dance with me?"

I turned around and looked at everybody when they starting laughing.

"Well, is you?"

"Yeah, yeah, Leo, I'll dance with your fine ass."

"When?"

"After I get in, you know, after a while."

Leo grabbed me by my hand. "Forget that. I been trying to get all this up on you for the longest. You dance now. The rest of y'all punks wait until I get back."

I could hear Jalen and them calling her my pimp and laughing. I'm not going to lie. Right at the moment, I felt like she was. Leo not only took me downstairs in the red lights where everybody was partying, she got me on the dance floor and was humping me like a dog for three straight songs. Then she whispered to me that she wasn't wearing panties.

I finally talked her into letting my boys in, but she made me promise to slow-dance with her as soon as the DJ slowed it down.

I went to let my boys in the party then told them to stand around me. "Look, y'all keep Leo the hell away from me the rest of the night."

"Man, if I see her, I'm goin' to bust her in the mouth for making me stand outside so long," Granger said. We knew he was joking. At least, we hoped he was.

I finally had a chance to kick back and see who was in the party. I noticed mostly a bunch of ol' heads up in there, but it was cool, because the get-together had a mixture of ages, and enough food, drink, and smoke for whoever wanted to get down. Jalen made sure I stayed away from the weed and drink but made sure I went to work on the food, while Granger and Maddox did their thing.

I felt a hand tug at the back pocket of my Sean John jeans.

"What's up, big baller? Why didn't you tell me you was coming out this way?" Katrina was wearing black shorts that showed off all her curves.

I let her know that we were just bouncing around, and the party was where we ended up.

Katrina was high and wasn't even trying to hide it. She went and got me a beer, and after Jalen took it from me while I sat on a stool, she backed up against me like some kind of experienced stripper in the club.

After a while I couldn't take anymore and decided I wanted to break her off for the very last time, because of Tori. I grabbed her by the hand, and we were moving out toward Jalen's car, where we had done some things before.

But the music stopped, and I heard someone calling me out.

"I hear the number one high school basketball player and future pro ballplayer is up in here! I said, I heard the number one player in the nation is here!"

Katrina stopped and looked up at me as I looked back and saw Toy standing in the middle of the party holding a drink.

"I want y'all to know something, and it's good that Langston is up in here, so he can't say I'm going behind his back talking trash about him. I want y'all to know, so you can make sure this bit of news travels as quick as the news, that the young'un is going to play ball overseas then on to the NBA."

The lights in the basement had been turned on, and it became extra quiet. Jalen moved away from the girl he had his arm around and in no time was standing next to me, just in case something was about to jump off.

Toy was buzzing off something, but nobody in the party cared because most of them were high too.

"Now ask him if I'm lying. I offered my services to the young buck, to be his agent and help him take on all this celebrity he's about to endure, but the truth of the matter is, L don't want nobody from the hood making deals for him and getting him as much money as he could possibly get."

It felt like more eyes were on me than at the state championship when I hit the winning basket at the buzzer.

"So when you out and about and his name come up like I know it will, 'cause we ain't had a player so good around since I came out of school, just run and tell that for me. Run and tell."

There was no way I was going to let Toy loud-talk me. That was something I didn't let happen anywhere.

"Look, man, if this how you get down, Toy, I'm cool with it. It still don't change things. I ain't messing with you, man, a'ight."

Then Jalen stepped in. "'Cause, you foul player. Why would L wanna put his business in jeopardy to mess with you anyway? Tell me that. We might as well get back to this party."

Toy looked around and smiled. He must have counted the numbers. I had way too many people up in there who would have stomped his drunk butt if he started beef. He stumbled to his seat with some girl he was with. I then whispered in Jalen's ear to come out to the car in about and hour, so we could get out of there and go home.

It took us longer than usual to have sex. Katrina, for some reason, wanted to have unprotected sex. I wasn't feeling that and told her I was going to put on a condom, if we were having sex at all. She was upset with my decision, which was strange, because condoms had always been the rule with her.

When we were finished and sitting in the backseat, waiting for Jalen to come out, Katrina said in the darkness, "Did you like that, *L?*"

"Yeah, it was cool." I was paying extra attention in the darkness to see if Jalen was on the way out while she put on her clothes.

"So when am I gonna see you again?"

"I don't know. I have a lot of things I need to do before I leave."

"Well, you goin' to send for me to come see you, right?"

A gang of peeps came out the house, and I tried to focus through the darkness to see if Jalen was one of them.

"I don't know. I mean, I doubt it, Katrina. This right here might be the last time we get the chance to hang out."

Putting on her shirt, Katrina said, "What you mean by that? Last chance?"

"I'm saying, it's just time I move on with my life."

"And what? You're not going to see me anymore?"

"How can I do that when I won't even be here? Plus" I stopped telling her what was on my mind because I didn't like the look on her face.

"Plus what?" She hit me on the arm. "Plus what?"

"I'm getting married. I'm taking Tori with me, and we're getting married."

Katrina smacked me across the face. "Married?"

I grabbed her hand. "You better watch yourself."

"What the hell you talking about getting married, Langston? I mean, you treating me like a ho or something."

"What's your problem?"

"My problem is that you just wanna run in and out of me like you own me or something then throw me away like yesterday's garbage."

"Look, I don't know what you want. All we been doing is hanging out and having sex. Katrina, you have never been my girl, so I don't know what your beef is."

She said, "You know what?"

"What?"

"That stuff Toy said about you in there is true. You don't care about nobody but yourself."

"Yeah, right. Nobody tells me how to run my life, or who I can or can't be with."

"I don't know why you wanna be with that bitch Tori for anyway? Everybody know you ain't getting none."

I got out the car then looked back in the seat at her. "Maybe that's the reason why."

Chapter Eleven

Tears in the Ghetto

Things started to move hella fast and I had no choice other than to take everything in stride or just freak out under all the pressure everybody was starting to put on me. I had a few interviews with major sports writers back to back to back. After that, a rep from a sports agency called and asked if I would keep them in mind after giving me his two-hour spiel. One hundred and twenty minutes was a long time, but I respected this guy and his agency because they weren't like Toy, pushy and stressing me to sign for all the wrong reasons. I was sure I was going to get picked up overseas, but I passed on the agency because I wanted to keep the last option of going to college in the bag.

I went to work out at three, and when I finished, I went over Tori's to let her mother know I was serious about marrying her. Of course my mother was all for it when I told her, and she made me promise I would treat Tori right and remember what she had gone through alone while raising me.

Then there was the party.

"What you mean, you don't wanna go, *L*?" Jalen's eyes were extended, his head moving from side to side.

"I don't know, man, I just don't."

"Look, *B*, this is your farewell party, your I'm-going-to-the-league bash." He lowered his voice and rose it as he spoke. "Our graduation party, boy!"

"I know all that, man, but this pressure is getting on me."

"You need to drop all of that. Just dump it in the trash. Do you know how many people would like your problems?"

I guess I did. He didn't have to remind me I was just looking at everything I needed to do and things I would need to get done before it was time to go. I knew it was pretty much a done deal that I was going to get taken by Barcelona, but I wanted to know the type of contract they were offering and make sure they knew I wanted to play no more than two years before I went to the NBA.

Jalen was on his job though. He had already been looking on the Internet for places to stay once we went overseas. Added to that, he called his cousin, a tailor who had a store down on Mt. Vernon Avenue, and gave him our sizes to make suits for graduation and when we finally met with Barcelona.

I woke up around nine. I wanted my mom to go to the party with me, but she wasn't having it. Said she wasn't trying to listen to any music about pumping and grinding with a bunch of young bucks who didn't know the difference between a cassette deck and an album cover.

I have to give props, the party was off the chain. Jalen did his thing, and everybody up in that piece was feeling the party. I don't know how Jalen did it, but he set the party up on the courts in The Vil, straight-up gansta-like. He had a banner with my picture on it, along with his name and Tori's, along with my mom's with **Congrats and good luck** written in bold letters.

All the love I was getting was genuine, and it felt good. It was like, with each handshake and hug, I was being given strength from others, like a ray of hope to fulfill dreams that other people had wished they would one day live. At first it was cool. But it started to mess with my head, because so many people were telling me how blessed I was and how I better make them all proud. I definitely didn't want to let anyone down, including myself, so I started to think about everything I needed to do again while looking out at everyone enjoying the party.

I did notice Tori change a bit though. Most of the time

when females came up to me to talk, she would either turn her head in the opposite direction, or just talk to one of her girls, like the situation didn't faze her.

I have to admit, what made me want to kick it with Tori was, she wasn't jealous or worried about any other female around because she knew she had the total package and I wasn't going anywhere. Tori would always tell me how she and a few of her girls always tripped off on the females at school who wanted to play like they were married then get upset when they found out that their men were messing around. Tori was truthful with hers and knew it was virtually impossible for a high school guy to be faithful to another girl, and if he was, she thought he was being very naïve.

But that night she had changed her game up and didn't care who knew about it because we were going to get married. Every single female who came up to talk to me, she made sure she either spoke to them or they recognized she was there holding my hand. It was funny, because most of them never knew Tori to act like that; she acted like she didn't care. The days of her turning her head away while other females flirted with me were over. My girl was checking any and everybody who stepped to me and disrespected her.

Katrina had walked up from behind the car, and Jalen, sitting around with three females on the trunk of the car, saw her peep game first. He called my name out to draw my attention to the situation. "L, L," he sang.

When I looked back, I noticed her strutting over with the walk she knew she had perfected. Katrina was a hood rat and didn't give a damn who knew it. She just smiled as some of the guys mentioned how her body was banging. Katrina was speaking loud and hadn't even opened her mouth yet.

She poked me in the stomach then said, "Hey, L."

"Hey, what's up?" I kind of figured she was 'bout to start some drama because of what I'd told her the night before.

Tori was sitting next to me on my other side. "Hey, Katrina," she said. Then she looked at her to see what she wanted.

"So, what's up, *L*? We goin' to kick it tonight when this slow down or what?"

I looked down at Katrina, trying to tell her with my eyes not to start because I really didn't want to flow with her on that negative vibe 'cause we was having a good time.

Tori snapped right in. "No, I don't think so. He's goin' to be with me tonight and every night after we get *married*."

Katrina paused for a moment and scanned Tori up and down. "Yeah . . . I heard," she sang out.

Tori smiled then looked out at the crowd when the DJ ripped her song "on the ones and twos."

I thought it was squashed, until Katrina opened her mouth again.

"Yeah, he told me right after we were together."

Jalen knew what kind of drama Katrina always liked to get started, so he had moved over close by. "Ohh, see, c'mon now. Don't start, Katrina, a'ight," he pleaded.

"I ain't worried about her, Jalen," Tori said. "I ain't never tried to stop *L* from going up inside her. The only thing I always asked of him was to wear protection, and he already told me he never did anything with you anyway without wearing a jimmy, sometimes two to be extra, extra safe, 'cause you neva know."

Jalen snickered a bit, and Katrina didn't like it.

"So what you sayin', Tori?"

"I'm saying he was going through the motions, 'cause, in my book, it ain't real like that."

Katrina put her hand up then back down like she was playing imaginary ping-pong. "How do you know what's real from what isn't? It's not like you have ever been with anybody anyway."

Tori smiled at her. "Sure haven't. But I tell you this— When I do, he's goin' in without the hat."

I looked at Tori, and she kissed me on my cheek.

Jalen was in the background, instigating and agitating like he does best. "I heard that," he mumbled.

Katrina yelled, "Look, you don't know a damn thing about me, so you need to just shut the hell up!"

"Oh, I know this about you, Katrina. I know for the longest I've been letting you play number two 'cause I just don't believe in giving up the goodies before marriage. Put it like this— L already done worn you out. He had permission. I'm goin' to be wifey, okay, and handling all his needs from now on, but good looking out, and I hope he saved some for the next one who run up in you."

I don't know why, but Katrina looked at me.

"So, is that how it is, L?"

I felt Jalen looking at me. Then Tori.

"Yeah, that's exactly how it is. I already told you."

"Oh, all right. Forget both of y'all!" Katrina said then stormed away.

Jalen pointed to the girls he was sitting next to. "See, that should be a lesson to all of you. Stop running around here boning everybody who you think like you. Keep those legs shut, you hear me? It will pay off. Just ask my girl Tori."

Tori ran off with her girl Kelly to get some grub at a Waffle House about an hour before I jumped in the car with Jalen to go meet up with them. We hadn't even been in the car five minutes before my phone rang. It was Kelly, and she was crying.

"Kelly, what's up?"

"Tori."

"What about her?"

Kelly was crying so much, I could barely understand her. I turned the music in Jalen's car all the way down.

"I'm at the hospital," she wailed, "and my head hurts so bad."

"The hospital? Tell me what happened. Kelly, where is Tori?"

Kelly was hysterical by now. "Langston, I don't know where she is. We were stopped at a light on Livingston and Nelson, and they jumped in our car and snatched her."

"What? Who snatched her? Kelly, what're you talking about?"

"I don't know who. When I woke up, I was coming into the hospital. I don't know where Tori is."

We were on the freeway next to the exit that put us where Kelly said she was. When I pointed to the exit, Jalen slammed on the gas from the far left lane, maneuvered through traffic, and zoomed down the hill to the exit without flinching. I don't know how he made it without getting us killed or causing a major pileup. We couldn't get all the way down the ramp to Livingston, so we jumped out the car and ran all the way down to see what was going on.

Police cars were everywhere, and we stood looking at Kelly's car, which was smoking and looked as though it was in some sort of movie scene.

"Damn! *L*, who shot up Kelly's car like that?"

"I don't know." My heart was pumping faster than it ever had for a basketball game.

You could hear in Jalen's voice how worried he was. "You see Tori anywhere?"

I didn't. I pulled up the yellow tape over my head and walked over with Jalen closer to the car.

"Hey, you guys have to get back," some thick-neck police officer told us.

"Look, I need to find out what happened to the other girl who was riding in this car."

"No. What you need to be doing is what I tell you," he said. "Now get your asses behind that tape."

Another officer walked up toward us. He looked familiar, but nothing was clicking in my mind but Tori and where she was. "Aren't you, Holiday? Langston Holiday? The ballplayer from East going pro?"

"Yeah, that's me." I was looking around at all the commotion, listening to him, but not really listening.

"Yeah, I remember you. I coached the team you played against every Saturday at the YMCA, PAL, when you were a young'un," he said.

"Sir, look, my girl was riding in this car. I need to find out what happened to her." I couldn't believe all the bulletholes in the car.

"Well, that's what we're trying to find out, son. Maybe you should go with me to the car and try to straighten this out."

Jalen went with me to the officer's car, and we answered questions about what we knew about what was going on. Which was, not a damn thing. I started to get mad when the officer started asking me and Jalen where we were when the shooting went down, and if I or Jalen were having any beef with the girls. Jalen told the man he wasn't answering any more questions like that, and I agreed.

When Officer Cummings saw that there was nothing he could get from us, that's when he started to help. He took us to get Jalen's car, and we followed him to the hospital to see Kelly to find out what she knew.

By the time we got there, Tori's people had already been there and gone out to the streets to search for her, since no one seemed to know what happened to her.

Kelly couldn't tell us anything. The only thing she told the police that she remembered was that they stopped at a light and out of nowhere her door was ripped opened and she saw a balled-up fist headed straight for her face, which knocked her out.

Officer Cummings told her that whoever shot up her

car didn't want to kill her because if they did, they could have easily done it.

I walked out the hospital with Jalen without a clue to what was going on. As always, Jalen became quiet when he was upset. I knew he was hurting like I was because he and Tori had always been like brother and sister.

"What we going to do, *L*?"

"I don't know, man. I mean, what can we do? Ain't no-body see nothing, and Kelly can't tell us anything."

"If they took her out the car, that means they wanted to take her someplace. Let's go back to The Vil and find out if anybody heard anything."

I wanted to go see my mother and Tori's people.

When I got home, my mother was on the couch. I didn't have to tell her anything. She already knew what was going on, and even though she was shaken, she was trying to make sure we were okay. She must have seen the anger in our eyes.

"Now you two ain't really been through nothing like this, so don't go out of here and get yourself into any trouble. The police is out there trying to find out where Tori is, and the more time you give them to look for her, instead of going out there and looking for somebody, like I know you want to do, it will give them a chance to find her."

"Yeah, but people ain't goin' to talk to no police," Jalen said. "Tori like family, and family need to take care of family, no matter who involved."

"Ma, we gotta at least go out and ride around and see what we see. I mean, ain't no way we staying up in here trying to wait to hear something."

"Well, what can I say? Y'all two are men now, but don't forget everything you got going for yourself, *L*."

"I won't," I told her.

"And I ain't going to let him," Jalen assured.

"But we gotta find her, Ma, we got to."

Our first stop was over Tori's to see her mom and sisters. I can't lie, I couldn't take it. I could hear the crying and the calling of Tori's name through the door before we even knocked. I stood on the step with Jalen and swear I was almost in tears, but I was trying to be strong before I knocked on that door.

Jalen wasn't able to keep the tears from flowing and was wiping his eyes every chance he got in case I got the strength to knock.

The courage wouldn't come to knock, so I backed away from the door.

As soon as we stepped away, the door opened. "Tori?"

It was her mom, and when she called out Tori's name, I could feel the pain she was going through.

We turned around.

"Oh, Langston, Jalen," she figured out.

"Ah, hey, we were just going to stop by to see how everybody was doing but thought we should give you a little bit more time before we came in," I told her.

"No, no, c'mon in," she said.

Jalen wiped his eyes and stopped before we went inside. "No, we gotta go find her, Ms. Hicks," he said. "That's what we should be doin' right about now, you know."

She tried to smile, but tears rolled down her face instead. "I know. I want to go out there too, but I'm afraid if I do, I'll miss her call. The police told me to just stay by the phone."

It was weird talking outside in the dark about Tori over all the nighttime action in The Vil that didn't stop for anything. The sirens were blaring, and people were on the hunt for whatever they were getting into.

I went over to Ms. Hicks and gave her a hug. I couldn't help but start to feel like Tori missing was my fault. As I had my arms around her while she cried, my mind went back to the day when were just freshmen and Tori's mom gave me the third degree about taking care of her and making sure she would always be safe when we were out. I wanted to tell her it was all my fault, that I would find Tori and bring her back home, but I wasn't so sure. We didn't have any kind of clues as to where she could be or what could have happened to her, and it was driving me crazy. So, as I held Ms. Hicks, I cried too.

Chapter Twelve
Hard-Pressed

It was hard to take, but three days had almost passed since Tori went missing. It was quiet all around The Vil, and I hadn't slept more than three hours straight since the night Tori was taken. The police didn't have any witnesses and didn't know anything. All they knew was that she was gone and that Kelly's car had been shot up. I heard they even questioned Katrina because of the beef she and Tori had right before Tori left. Katrina had all types of people speaking for her and stepping up to clear her name. I didn't think she had anything to do with it. Besides, her bark was always louder than her bite.

I was pissed because no one in the media was really saying anything about Tori missing like they do for those suburban girls when they get snatched up. I wasn't too young to know what it was about though. The media never cared about what went down in the hood and wasn't going to waste time on some young black girl, so I did what I could on that end. Out of the seven interviews I had concerning going pro, I told them what I was going through and made sure I talked about Tori because I wanted somebody to find my girl.

"C'mon, Langston, that shot's going to be your bread and butter when you come overseas," I heard Barcelona's head scout voice echo through the gym. "I can see it now. You're going to be hell to defend. Do you know how hard it was to play against Scottie Pippen back in the day? When you're floating around the elbow looking straight at the bucket we're going to want you to take it. It's what you're going to be known for on our team," the scout shouted.

I couldn't believe I kept shooting and missing it as the scout continued to run his mouth.

"Make it your signature, baby. Live it and love it!"

The traveling scout working me out was sitting in the bleachers next to Coach Pierce. It was my second workout in two days for Barcelona. I can't even front—I wasn't even impressing myself.

Coach showed up big though. He was my buffer between the scouts and the terrible workouts I was having. He pulled them aside to let them know my situation. He explained to them why my vertical had been forty-one inches instead of a consistent forty-six and the reasons my shooting touch was off. He knew Tori and understood what I was going through. There had been a few times when Coach didn't think he was reaching me during the season and he went to Tori to get into my head, and it worked every time. She was definitely in my head by this time, because I was worried to death about her.

I looked over toward the bleachers to Coach and the scout. "I'm sorry, but this just ain't going to work today. I need to find out what's going on with Tori. I shouldn't even be doing this right now."

The scout looked over at Coach then back at me. "Look, son, it's this simple. In the pros there is no time for a break when things are tough. We work on our game, get our heads right, and try as best as we can to do what we're paid to do. Ask any of the players when you meet them. It's how you become a star."

I couldn't tell if the scout knew, but Coach Pierce did, and he stiffened a bit.

He must have remembered the time when one of the assistants on our team tried the same take-one-for-the-team speech when my grandmother died and the entire team had to pull me off him. Coach put his hand up to silence me before I cussed the scout out.

"Look, Langston," the scout said, "listen to me. Things

will work out for the better. You have to believe that, son. Dig in and do what we've seen you do in the state championships and on tape in your all-star summer league games. I want you to have a good workout, so I can go back and tell my people that you'll be worth all the money you'll be paid."

I stood there looking at Coach and the scout, along with the side exit to the streets, with the ball up under my arm. I had major thoughts running through my head. Should I tell this baldheaded Dick Vitale look-alike to kiss the bottom of my shoes and come back another day, or should I stay on the court like a piece of meat and let him evaluate my skills like he came to do in the first place? I don't know why, but I didn't like the way Coach and the scout were looking at me while I stood there. It made me feel like a slave on the block getting ready to get sold or something. I took a deep breath and gutted it out though. I just let their looks and stares motivate me and gave them what they wanted to see.

Afterward, the scout was all smiles. He shook my hand like a groupie then told me he would be in touch later that night.

Jalen walked in about five minutes later. "How'd it go?" he asked, his voice echoing throughout the gym.

"A'ight. Said he was gonna call me tonight."

Jalen put three or four balls back on the rack, grabbed my towel then threw it to me.

I knew right away something wasn't right with him. It was written all over his face. "What? What's wrong? They find Tori?"

He dropped his head and took a deep breath.

"What is it, Jalen? What's wrong?" I walked over to him. "Talk, J."

"Toy just stopped me in The Vil."

"And?"

"He say he can get Tori back."

"What you mean, get her back?"

"That's what he sayin'."

"That means she ain't dead, right?"

"He just say he can get her back. Didn't say if she was dead or not."

My mind just wanted to explode. "C'mon, Jalen, tell me what you're talking about!"

"Toy made it clear he didn't have anything to do with her getting snatched up, but he can get her back to us, if you sign with him."

"Sign?"

Jalen nodded.

"He said that? Oh, hell no. That scandalous bastard." With the quickness, I started to think about a way to hurt Toy and get Tori back.

"C'mon, L, don't even think about it. Toy said he knew you, L. Said you go to the police talking smack, and he'll deny saying a word. Then he say, if you get a gang of peeps to come after him, he's not going to say a word, and we may never see her again."

"So what he want then?"

"You to sign. Make him your agent for three years and he has full control of your career."

"He said that?"

"Every word."

What could I do? If Toy knew where Tori was, I wanted to know too. It didn't matter to me if we found her dead or alive. Of course, I wanted little mama alive because that was my baby, but if we found her dead, at least we knew. It was a terrible-ass way to think, but I wanted to know. I needed to know.

"So when he wanna do this?"

"You're going to do it?"

"What else can I do? Man, forget Toy! I'll sign with him and get Tori back then fire him."

"Said he wants to meet tonight, eleven thirty on the court in The Vil."

Eleven thirty couldn't come fast enough for me. I wanted Tori back, and I didn't tell a soul what I was up to because those were Toy's instructions that came out of Jalen's mouth. All I wanted to do was get Tori back to her mother and take good care of her.

Jalen came by to pick me up. He was focused. We both were. We went out to The Vil about an hour before things were going to go down to talk about what we were going to do once we had Tori. Jalen wanted so bad to tell Tori's mom about what was happening, but we decided not to. If they even knew Toy could tell them something about Tori being missing, they would kill him before we ever got a chance to get her back. We were standing on the court waiting for Toy to show up. Jalen was facing one end; I was looking down at the other. All of a sudden the floodlights were snatched on, and I could see Toy walking toward us with a big-ass smile on his face. As usual he was wearing a silk shirt with dress pants and some Italian leather shoes. Three guys I had never seen before were walking behind him. They had snarls on their faces, but I didn't care if they wanted beef; they were going to get it.

Toy and his partners stopped, and Toy was looking me and Jalen over. "My brothers, let this be an example that your agent will never be late to a business meeting. "So how did your workout go today?"

"How'd you know about it?"

Toy snickered. "It's my job to know about it. I heard you had a bit of trouble starting off with your concentration, but then you got it going."

"If you knew, why'd you ask? And get over it, 'cause I didn't come to talk about it."

"Look, I know this is not how you wanted it to go down, L, but such is life. You goin' to see a lot of things happen in your life that you didn't plan."

"Save all that, man," I told him. "I'm doing this for one reason, and that's Tori."

Toy reached over to one of his boys and held out his hands. "By the way, these are my new friends from Harlem. They going to be traveling with you during the season."

"The hell they are," Jalen said. "If you didn't know, that's my job to make those kind of decisions, and your fake-ass P. Diddy bodyguards need to fall back to Harlem."

Toy laughed Jalen off. "Oh, is that how it's gonna be?

"It's already a done deal," I told him, "so you can get your boys to follow someone else."

Toy looked at his goons then at me and reached over and handed me the contract.

"Where do I sign?"

"Last page," he said. "You're not even going to read it?"

"I want Tori back."

"Well, let me give you a brief rundown. I get thirty percent. I get ten percent the first year, twenty the second, and thirty on the last."

"Thirty?" Jalen questioned.

"You heard right. You getting more than an agent. You're getting your fiancée back."

"I don't care. I just want her back."

Toy tossed me a pen, and Jalen moved in front of me so I could use his back to sign.

"And don't think you gonna sign the contract, find your girl, then fire me. Look at page three. I cannot be fired until my three years expire."

Jalen looked back at me. "I know the game, *L*. I told you that long ago."

I threw the contract back at Toy, and it hit the ground. "Where is she, Toy?"

"At the park on the East side, off Livingston, in an abandoned car."

"She alive?"

"Maybe, maybe not," he said before he picked up the contract. "My deal was to tell you where you could find her."

As we took off running for Jalen's car, I could hear Toy's voice in the background saying, "Call me later. We have some things we need to talk about—endorsements, the whole kit and caboodle, baby!"

Chapter Thirteen

Didn't You Know?

On a normal day with a chill drive and nothing pressing on the brain, the ride out to Livingston to the park was fifteen to twenty minutes max. But Jalen raised his hood hit the hots, and when it cranked, I stepped on the gas and we were rolling. Jalen didn't care about stop signs, traffic lights, or anyone who may have been in the street. We were on the real fast and furious to get Tori.

When we got to the park where there were two sections separated by a bridge, Jalen looked at me to find out what side to check first, and I pointed toward the nearest entrance. We had to make a quick sliding stop in the path that was lined with rocks because there was a link chain tied to two metal poles to stop cars going in after dark.

"Forget this!" Jalen said and smashed right through it.

The next thing I knew, we were on the other side of it and going down a winding, dusty road looking for Tori. We saw a car up ahead with headlights on and stopped behind it. We ran up to the car and looked in and saw a body laying face down. Then, all of a sudden, there was a scream, and we jumped back.

Up underneath the girl, a guy showed his face. "Yo', man what you guys doing out here?" He reached under his seat and pulled his pistol.

"Look, man, we ain't mean no harm, okay. I'm looking for somebody, and I thought she might be up in this car."

His eyes were squinted because Jalen's lights were burning the hell out of them. He went back and forth, pointing the gun at us. "You sure that's all this is?"

"Yeah, man, we're sure," Jalen assured him.

He looked at us again. "You see anything?"

"Like what?" Jalen wanted to know.

"What you looking for?" He looked at us again and put his pistol down.

We moved away from the car.

"There's nothing else around here, Jalen."

"Let's go over to the other side."

We ran to the car, and Jalen smashed on the gas and peeled out to the other side of the park, where we sat for a few minutes. Then, at the very end of the park, we noticed a car parked with the back end toward us.

"That's got to be Tori in there, Jalen."

"Yup."

"Pull all the way up, man, all the way up."

Driving up to the car was creepy. Jalen was driving slowly, and the rocks under the tires made the whole situation more intense. When Jalen stopped the car, we walked up to it and looked in. Tori was in the backseat with her eyes closed.

I opened the door. "Tori? Tori?"

"Is she dead, *L*?"

"Tori?" I called out like three times. I was scared to touch her, but I did anyway. Touched her face then put my hand on her chest to see if she was breathing. "Tori? Tori? Tori, are you okay? Tori, answer me, damn it!"

She finally responded. "*L*, is that you? *L* . . ."

"She's alive, *L*! She's alive! C'mon, man, pick her up and get her in the car!" Jalen shouted.

We were not wasting anytime trying to call an ambulance to take her to the hospital. She looked weak and was barely breathing and crying out for her mother and sisters.

She had her head on my lap in the backseat as Jalen pushed it hard to the hospital. I could barely hear Tori, but what I did hear, I didn't like at all. She kept saying they wouldn't stop, and when I looked down toward her legs, she had marks on the inside of her thighs that looked like razor cuts.

The hospital took her away from us right away.

When we went outside to move the car, there were close to thirty policemen pointing their guns at us, telling us to kiss the pavement. We did exactly what they told us.

By the time the police stopped asking us questions about how we found Tori, it was way over an hour later. We got back into the hospital and saw Tori's mom there, all of her sisters, my mother, and, of all people, Toy.

My mother stood up and gave me a hug when we walked into the waiting room. "Boy, are you all right?"

"Yeah, Ma, I'm cool."

"Langston, why didn't you call us to let us know where you were going? You could have been hurt out there."

"We didn't have the time," Jalen let her know. "All we wanted to do was get Tori back."

"Boys ain't never listened to me, since you walked all the way to Carl Brown IGA together when you were five years old to get them damn cream pies."

Tori's mother stood up and gave us a hug. She was so happy that Tori was still alive. When I asked how Tori was doing, she didn't tell me more than I already knew. Tori was weak and barely breathing, but the doctors said that she would make it and put her in intensive care, just in case.

I moved over into the corner with Jalen. "Yo', we not letting this slide," I told him.

"Oh, hell to the naah. I'm already on it, L. Ain't no way we letting Tori get played like this."

"Did you see all those cuts on her?"

"Somebody took a razor to her. She's in pain."

"Well, when I find out who did it, they ain't going to know what pain is."

"L, we going to find out, okay, but when we do, you

need to step back on it. You don't need to know what happens or when it happens 'cause it's going to be on the gruesome tip."

I didn't want to hear what Jalen was saying, but I knew he was only watching out for me and my future, like he'd always done.

"Yeah, yeah, okay."

Toy decided to interrupt us. "What I tell you," he said. "My word is bond."

"What you want, Toy?" I asked him.

"I'm your agent, so I don't need to want a gotdamn thing to come talk to you. You are my responsibility, but at the moment, I have something for you. Here is your copy of your contract. Keep it in a safe place."

I snatched it out of his hand and gave it to Jalen to hold for me.

"Look, if I find out you had anything to do with Tori getting hurt, I'm going to—"

"Listen, your young ass is starting off on the wrong foot," Toy said, cutting me off. "You know I don't get down like that. And please don't ask me to reveal who told me where you could find her. You know the code in the street, and that's the code we living by on this one."

"Yeah, I got your code," I told him.

"Mmm-hmm. That's what I thought," he snarled. "Now, listen, the overseas draft is little less than two weeks away. I need to sit down and talk to you about some things before that time."

I just gave him a blank stare.

"Look, I know we got started off on the wrong foot but, young buck, believe me—You done signed, and your ass need to go pro now. There is no turning back. You got that?"

I didn't like it, but Toy was right. My plans to keep college an option were gone. I had signed with an agent and I had to play overseas. I had to do me in a big way now, and I had to play the game. "Yeah, I got it," I said back.

Toy looked over at Jalen. "What about you?"

"Just do your job and get out of my face."

"But I'm still calling the shots, Toy. You understand that? Any and everything that goes down is my call," I let him know.

"No doubt," Toy said.

"So, Toy, what brings you over? I didn't know you were so into things happening in the family."

I guess our little meeting in the waiting room was way too much for my mother not to be included.

"Reecy, now you know I'm always concerned when your boy needs some support. Besides, didn't L tell you the good news?"

My mother looked up at me and Jalen turned his back as if looking in another direction. "What news?"

"He signed with me today," Toy said. "I'm your son's new agent."

Chapter Fourteen

Runnin' Thangs

I spent as much time as I could in the waiting room hoping Tori would get enough strength to really talk to me. I was only getting about four hours of sleep each night. Because nothing is ever written in stone until the final contract is signed, Toy set up workouts for several other overseas teams just in case something went wrong with Barcelona.

On the day of another workout, I woke up smelling breakfast.

"Ma, thanks for the food."

"Mmm-hmm."

I looked over at her. She was sitting watching television on the couch, but the kitchen was so close, I could see her just fine.

"You want to come out to my workout today? I'm 'bout to bust that ass today."

"No, thank you."

"What? Why not?"

"I didn't think you wanted me around in your business dealings anymore."

"What do you mean?"

"How could you sign with that fool, Toy?"

"It was just something I had to do."

It was the very first time I hadn't been honest to my mother about my basketball career, and I didn't feel good about it. I didn't want to get her involved, though, because getting Tori back was the reason I signed the agreement, nothing more. If my mother had found out that Toy blackmailed me, she would have gone to see him with that little pistol she kept in her nightstand. I didn't think it was worth getting her in trouble, so I just decided to keep why I signed with Toy on the hush.

"Had to do? What do you mean by that?"

"It was just something I decided to do. Ma, look, Toy's been around. He knows a few people in the league. Plus, the pressure was starting to get to me. It's only a three-year deal."

"But I don't like him, Langston. Toy has been in some scandalous mess around here, and by the way, I see it. He hasn't changed that much."

By the time I finished talking to my mother, she eased a bit. I promised her I wouldn't let him ruin my career, and that things would be okay, but she still didn't like that I'd signed with Toy.

Jalen came over to take me out to the gym, and my mother put a smile on her face, and decided to come along. She hated riding in Jalen's car. She kept asking him, "If you have to start the car like that, how do you turn it off?"

It was good to hear her giving Jalen attitude. Things were getting back to normal.

I wanted to see Tori for a quick second before I went into the gym, so Jalen swung around to the hospital first.

"What do you mean, she doesn't want to see him?" Jalen asked the nurse after they wouldn't let me back to Tori's room.

"She has a list of people she doesn't want to see at the moment, and Langston Holiday is on the list."

My mother asked to see the list, and the nurse gave it to her. "Well, my name isn't on it. Let me go see her. I'll be right back."

About twenty minutes later, she came back.

I could tell she had been crying. "Ma, what's up?"

"She just needs some time, *L*."

"She doesn't want to see me?" I started to move toward her room.

My mother grabbed my arm. "Baby, she can't right now."

"Why not?"

"She was raped."

I almost fainted. "Raped?"

"Yes, she's not well, and she doesn't want to see any men right now."

I felt a tear fall down my face. "Not even me? She don't want to see me?"

After my mother explained to me what happened to Tori, there was no way I was going to work out for the scout. All my energy was sucked out of me, and I felt paralyzed and unable to think about anything I needed to be doing. All that rah-rah, go-get-them bull the scouts used to pump me up wasn't going to work.

I needed to get away, and that's exactly what we did.

"Man, she said it was at least ten of them, Jalen."

"L, I can't even imagine that happening to Tori. No wonder she don't want to see us."

We were sitting in Jalen's car. He had just scored some brew, and there was no way he was going to keep me away from drinking with him.

"It ain't right, man," I told him.

"As long as I have known Tori, the only person she has ever fucked with is me. 'Jalen, yo' car a mess. Jalen, leave those tricks alone. Jalen, where is your homework. My sister, man."

"Bad things always seem to happen to good people."

"I could care less about graduating now. I mean, she won't even be there."

"All those big plans," Jalen said with a faraway look. Then he drank down some brew.

"All Tori talked about was strutting across the stage like a model."

"You know she was going to do it, L. She was goin' to kill 'em. Hell, she ain't dead, but I'm pouring out for her. This her taste. This going to lift her up for real." Jalen took his beer and pointed it toward the sky then let a drop fall to the ground. "That's for you, girl!"

Out of nowhere Toy appeared and looked into the window of my side of the car. "You mind telling me what you two retards are doin'?"

"What it look like? We don't answer to you; you answer to us," I let him know.

"Roll up on us again like that, and I'm telling you, you're not going to like what happens," Jalen told him. "I think he need to get that straight, L, or nothing ever going to get done in this camp."

Toy began to laugh, but his smile was fake, and then it turned into a snarl. "You muthafuckas don't know anything, do you? If you haven't realized, no matter how you want to slice and dice it, I'm the leader of this bitch. I am the one making the deal for your contracts. I'm the one talking on your behalf for endorsements. Fools, never bite the hand that feeds you. You got that?"

"Toy, I think you been drinking, man. I mean, I know I can't fire you for the next three years, but I tell you this—You can go get a deal with IBM, Gatorade, or Ford, and I don't have to sign a damn thing."

"True that, L," Jalen said, "but add Cadillac on his ass too, since he like to ride so nice." Jalen began to laugh. "So who really running things now, with your corny ass?" Then he took a sip of his beer, making an irritating slurping sound.

"Look, y'all young bucks think you something 'cause you got a few rappers and players in the league phone numbers on speed dial. But let me tell you something. Everybody know Toy. They know me 'cause I should have played in the league and gotten what I just got your ripe, young ass, Langston."

"Man, what are you talking about?" Jalen wanted to know.

"I'm talking about the seventeen-million-dollar shoe contract that's being faxed to my office as we speak."

Jalen sat up and burped after another sip of brew. "Seventeen million?"

I couldn't even talk. My tongue would not move.

Toy looked at me. "Now, mister man, be your ass funny and don't sign that."

Come to find out, Toy had made the deal with a bigwig up at New Funk Apparel who he'd roomed with in his college days. They were kicking off their new line and told him the only way they were going to reach the young urban market was to sign a baller who knew the streets and could relate to their brand. When I asked Toy why he didn't let me know about the deal in the works, he said he wasn't going to tell me about it when I wasn't signed to him, then give me the opportunity to go behind his back and broker a deal myself. And that's exactly what I would have done.

I just didn't trust Toy, but his deal was sweet, and it was a good first step to, at least, start giving him a little bit of credit.

We went home to tell my mother the news.

"Why y'all smiling so much?"

We were standing in the living room, and she was still working on some knitting or something she said she was going to sell on the streets.

"L and Jalen, if you don't tell me why those grins are on your faces, I'm goin' to—"

"Ma, you ain't going to believe this."

"No. What you two ain't going to believe if you don't get from in front of my TV is how much I can still spank that ass."

Jalen looked at me and started to laugh.

"Now what is it?"

"Ma, I just got offered a seventeen-million-dollar shoe contract!"

If I only had a camera to capture the look on her face.

Chapter Fifteen
You're My Girl

I flat out needed to tell Tori about the deal. I couldn't let her sit up in the hospital and think her life had been ruined, because the shoe deal meant we both were going to be set for life.

Toy was already celebrating. He sent a car for us to come over to his place to sign the contract, but I needed to see Tori first. I didn't care what it took, but I was getting up in that hospital room to my girl.

We had the driver park down the street from the hospital, so we wouldn't draw attention to the car. The driver started tripping, talking about he didn't want to sit in the hood in a limo. I could tell he was scared out of his mind. I probably would have been too. There were plenty of people in the streets that night, but I told him to lock the doors and get in the back and wait for us, and that's exactly what his scared ass did.

When we walked into the hospital, we went straight to the elevators and up to the floor Tori was staying on. We knew that the nurse station was right in front of the elevators, so the nurses could see everyone coming in and out. We didn't even talk about what we were going to do, but I knew, from coming up with Jalen, I was going to play off him and go with the flow.

When the elevator stopped, there were two nurses standing behind their station. One looked at us, and the other was busy checking a chart. We stepped out the elevator and there was no way we were going past the nurse, who was already looking at us like we were ready to start some problems. The good thing about it; they were not the same nurses who saw us earlier.

"May I help you?"

I looked down at Jalen.

"Ahh, yeah . . . I'm here to see Tori Hicks."

As soon as the nurse looking at the charts heard Tori's name, she got up all in our business and started barking at her coworker. "Check her list. You know she has a list," she snapped. "Plus, she was like an emergency case with no insurance, I might add, so admin wants to schedule to see her in the morning for payment, or we're going to have to send her home."

It was clear as a painting that the two nurses didn't like each other.

Jalen always had a knack for starting commotion. He said, "Damn! People don't even like to speak right to people anymore, do they?"

The nurse looked up from the list and smiled. "They sure don't, do they?" Then she looked over at her co-worker.

The evil nurse with the attitude looked over at Jalen then her co-worker and rolled her eyes at them.

"So what's your name?" Jalen asked. Already, his mind had turned this thing into trying to get into some jeans.

"Monique," she said, a flirty smile on her face.

Monique was fine in her nurse uniform. She had a short, black haircut, a real nice smile, and a whole bunch of body. There was no way Jalen was going to get any of that.

"So you sayin' she got some kind of list or something?" Jalen inquired.

The nurse with the attitude grabbed her chart and began walking away. "Yeah, it's a 'no admittance' list." Then she stormed off like she was mad at the world.

"Wow! You gotta work with her all night?"

I just smiled and let Jalen do his thing. All I wanted to do was get in to see my baby.

"All night, every night," she answered. "I can't believe they paired me up with that skank."

"Damn! If I had to work with her, she wouldn't be check-ing on rooms. Home girl would be in a room, because I would whup that ass, bust her all up," he joked.

The nurse thought Jalen was so funny. I couldn't believe she seemed to be feeling him.

"Look, my name is Norm, and this is Frank. I know he's tall and a li'l weird-lookin', but he cool. Our names are not on that list, right?"

Home girl skimmed down the list at rapid speed and looked back at Jalen and smiled. "No. You can go on back."

Jalen pushed me on my way then winked his eye at me. "Frankie, you go 'head. I want to talk to Monique for a minute."

Tori's last name was handwritten on the door on a small card. The door was cracked open, but the room was dark, except for the television. I smoothed out my gear and put like three sticks of gum in my mouth. Tori hated when I drank beer with-out her, and trust, I had been.

I opened the door and slid inside. There was only one bed, and Tori looked like she was lying on her side, her back to the television, so it was watching her. I didn't know what the hell to do.

I took a few steps toward her then stopped. I was look-ing down at her when the television set turned off, leaving me standing in the darkness looking over her. It must have been on automatic shut-off.

"Hi, L," Tori said in a voice so weak.

I smiled a little. "Girl, how'd you know it was me?"

"I know you be rockin' that Cool Water, that's how." She turned over in my direction very slow.

I stood there for a minute before saying anything. "You want me to get the lights?"

"No, no, leave them off, okay."

I still hadn't moved closer to the bed yet. "So how you doing? You feeling better?"

She waited before she answered. "I guess. What's up with you?"

"Just been tryin' to get in here to see you, that's all."

"L . . ."

"Baby girl, don't say nothing, a'ight. Ma, told me everything, okay."

I wanted to hit myself in the mouth when I heard Tori begin to cry. I stood there a while longer without a word, but I didn't want her to scream and tell me to get out. I had to change it up quick.

"Tori, guess what?"

"Mmm-hmm."

"You ready for some good news?"

Tori tried to gather herself. "I guess."

"Well, listen to this. In a few minutes, I'm going to sign a seventeen-million-dollar shoe endorsement contract."

When she answered me back, it didn't seem as though she cared. Her voice was flat, dull, and groggy. "That's good, L. I always knew it was going to happen for you."

I took one step closer to the bed and finally could see my girl's eyes. I then tried to smile, but the razor cut marks on her face came close to making me cry. "Girl, what you mean, happen for me? This is happening to us."

"You don't have to say that you know."

"Why not? It's the truth."

"'Cause, 'cause of what happened to me." Tori rolled herself into a ball.

"It didn't just happen to you. It happened to me too, and everybody else who loves you, Tori. We all going to be okay."

"You're saying all that now, L."

"That's right. I'm saying it now, and I'm going to be saying it forever."

Tori looked at me. "Really, L?"

"You are my wifey, okay? What do I have to do to make you believe that?"

Tori didn't answer.

I wasn't leaving.

She finally looked at me the way she used to, and I sat down on the bed, and she reached up to me, and I held her until she stopped crying.

Chapter Sixteen

Raise Yo' Glass

After spending some time with Tori, I was ready to take on the world. I made her promise me she would tell those fools in the hospital that I could come see her anytime I felt like it.

Meanwhile, Jalen got ol' girl's phone number at the nurse booth then came in the room and tried to make Tori promise she was going to walk the stage with us like we all had planned for graduation. Tori didn't know if she was going to be up to it and said if she could, she would.

Jalen stood around and told a few jokes until she laughed. Then we left.

We finally showed up over Toy's. He had a loft over on the East side. It was a nice one. You could tell he had some work done on it, and when we walked in and I saw all the artwork on the walls, it gave me an idea to get my mother a house and fill it up with artwork.

There were like thirty or forty people over Toy's. I was surprised to see them there, because the only thing I planned on doing was looking over the contract, signing it, and getting my million-dollar advance on the deal, minus Toy's and Jalen's cut. But Toy had other plans. He wanted to party.

"Here is really the reason we all gathered up in my spot tonight!" Toy yelled when we walked through the door. First, he reached out to shake my hand. Then he moved in quickly and gave me a hug, then Jalen. "Because you know if we didn't have nothing to celebrate y'all wouldn't be up in here drinking up all my expensive drink. Give these two brothers a hand and then excuse us for a minute."

Everyone started to applaud us.

Toy took us in his living room that had these old antique doors with paned windows. He slid them back, and we walked in.

He looked at me then Jalen. "How's everything goin'?"

"We cool," I told him.

Jalen just nodded.

"C'mon . . . y'all going to have to let me in. I mean, gotdamn, we 'bout to sign this deal for sev-en-teen mil, baby! You not pleased with my work or what?"

"I guess, man, this all new to us, Toy. All I wanna do is play ball and take care of my mother and my girl."

Toy stopped from sipping on his drink. "So how's she doing? Your girl?"

I looked at Toy hard, trying to look through his face and glazed over eyes to see if he had anything to do with Tori getting raped. "She a'ight."

"Yeah, she a soldier. She going to be all right," Jalen told him.

"Then good. You all set then. We can sign this contract, fax it back, and by tomorrow, our money going to be in your separate account."

"Separate account? What account we talking about?"

"The one your father—"

"My father?"

"Yeah, he came over and told me he already set one up for you. Wait a minute." Toy walked over to his desk and handed me a package.

"What's this?"

"Hell, if I know. Like I say, your pops stopped by here and gave it to me to give to you. Said some bull like, he doesn't trust me, and make sure you get this. You got the whole damn family hating me, *L.*"

"Look, he ain't family, a'ight."

"Well, he sounded like family to me."

I took the package from Toy and opened it up. It was a piece of paper with a bank account with my name on it. There was a note attached—*Son, don't ever let Toy put any of your money in his account. Watch your money around him. Always verify what he does. I know I haven't been in your life like I should, but at least take my advice.*

I looked over to Jalen then put the note back into my package and stared Toy down again.

"So you straight?" Toy wanted to know.

"Yeah, we good. Now, where do I sign?"

Toy took me over to his oak desk and swore to me that this would not be the last endorsement deal we would sign together. He said he looked it over and everything was legit. Then he started bragging about his law degree, and how he was glad he'd finished school so he could do his thing with his new agency.

I told Toy to leave me and Jalen alone while we looked things over. I took my time reading the contract, which was thorough and had all kinds of restrictions, like being associated with drugs and any criminal activity, which would automatically terminate my contract.

"So what you thinking, *L?*" Jalen wanted to know as he paced around Toy's office, looking at certificates and diplomas on his wall.

"Man, it's right here on paper. They want me to pimp their brand, Jalen. Photo shoots for magazines, lace them up on the court if I want. And there's a bonus if the product takes off and I decide to sign on the clothing line they are going to have off the ground after next season. What do you think?"

"I think you should sign then"—Jalen looked into the party—"But after three years, *L*, I want to get you away from this slimy-ass Toy. I mean, I don't trust him, and I damn sure don't like the fact that somebody came to him to tell us where Tori was."

"True that." I put my arm around Jalen. "But we got her back now. And after I sign this and my contract to play ball, we don't even have to take his calls. We'll just string him out."

"Unless he comes through big again," Jalen said.

"Exactly. Then we'll just cash the check."

"And string his ass out a li'l more."

It was like two in the morning when I finished reading the contract. Toy said he didn't care and called his old roommate then faxed the signed contract back to him. Toy put him on the phone. I vaguely remembered his name when he played basketball. He averaged nine points a game but was more interested in business than basketball during his playing days.

I felt good about signing after talking to him. He at least brought a little cred to Toy's crooked ass.

The party was still going strong after we sent the fax. Everyone was having a good time, and by the time I looked around, Jalen had him a plate of food.

For a long time I was used to being the center of attention of peeps my age, but this was different. I was standing amongst grown folk fifteen, twenty years older celebrating what had happened to me, and it felt good.

All of a sudden Toy asked everyone to gather around in a circle around me.

"Listen up. I know I'm a little bit drunk. Okay, you're right, I'm tore up. But this feels good, don't it? This is special because a lot of people have played ball that we know, especially us being old heads now. We've had a few pro players. There have been so many who never had the chance, but if given the right grooming and opportunity would have made it to the league, just like Langston Holiday is going to do. So, saying all that, I want to pay homage to the ballplayers who have went on to the pros and those who have laid the legacy down in Columbus of fine ballplayers, you know, the brothers who have given us the chance to see the best basketball in the country. So, what I would like to do is just go around the room and everybody just hold up your glasses and let's salute whoever comes to your mind who brought heat on the courts in our city. The ballplayers that we know and love that have paved the way for my man Langston Holiday to become what he is today."

Everything was quiet, except for was a funky jazz tune playing by Miles Davis. I heard Toy mention some homie named Foley, the bass player making it come to life like there was no tomorrow. Toy pointed to the first person to his right, and everyone just started naming legends of the city who could all ball.

Hearing all the names brought back to memory stories I had heard coming up, and I became choked up. It gave me another reason to promise myself I would not let their legacy down, because it lived through me.

The first person said, "Dewey Milton."

The next said, "Gregg Bell."

The next, "Rocky Craft."

And they just went on and on mentioning names, including, Curtis Craft, Todd Penn, The Davis Twins, Robert Tatum, Hank Cornley, Adam Troy, Eric Troy, Terry Poindexter, Herb Williams, Samaki Walker, Bruce Howard, Bob Harris, Randy Clarkson, Charles Jones, Paul O'Neil, Tino Richards, Phillip Miller, Kenny Battle, Daryl Delaney, Roy Bobo, Reggie Rankin, Lawrence Funderburke, Eric Hilton, Marvin "Bean" Walker, Eric Shepard, Nate Harris, Mike McKinney, Troy Hitchcock . . . .

Chapter Seventeen

All Mine?

Graduation came and went so quickly, I didn't really believe it was going down. It was just like I thought it would be—a lot of people happy as hell they could move on with their lives, others crying and so confused to what was really going on, they could have used another year of classes.

Tori showed up though. She called me that morning after we sat up in her hospital room almost all night begging her to walk across the stage with us.

Jalen drove to the hospital. I walked inside, pulled out a wad of cash and paid all her bills, then rolled her right out of there and into Jalen's ride. We had talked about this day since freshman year, but we didn't expect to be paid and rolling in a brand-new, sparkling Escalade.

The Escalade was Jalen's. He took his piece of the cut from my shoe contract for being my handler and went out and bought a smoking black one with all the tricks, including the spinners, that put Toy's to shame. Plus, he got all of us cell phones, including my mom, that worked on the same network, so we could stay in touch at all times. He even had the nerve to be calling his business Black Ice Management Inc.

With the overseas draft coming up, I had things I needed to handle because, once the season started, there was no way I could concentrate on anything else. So, instead of letting my mother go out and find a house on her own, I went out and did it for her, to ease my mind and make sure she was okay while I was away.

***

"So, why are we standing up in this place?" She was look-ing around.

"'Cause, Ma, this is your house," I said to her. "Now the question is, When you goin' to put some furniture up in here? 'Cause I need to rest my legs."

"Boy, what're you talking about?"

I nudged my girl. "Tell her, Tori."

Tori was smiling, but when she realized everyone was looking at her, she backed off. She was still working herself back to her groove.

I put Tori under my arm and walked over to the marble fireplace, and my girl got some confidence up in her with the quickness. "Well, since you were taking forever to find a house and won't move over to Easton like *L* wanted you to, he bought you this house, close but not too close to the hood."

My mother stared at me speechless.

"And," I added, "by being here, you can still know what goes down in The Vil with all your hood rat friends, 'cause you only ten minutes away."

"You actually bought this house, boy?"

"Sure did."

Mom was looking around, and her voice echoed. "This house probably cost seven hundred thousand dollars!"

"Mom, it's okay. You act like I'm broke or something. I have wanted you out The Vil as long as I remember, and you're moving up in here, tonight."

"Tonight?"

"Yup."

"What about all my stuff?"

"What about it? Just leave it."

"I'm not leaving all my furniture back there."

Jalen walked out the kitchen on cue then flipped his cell off. "It'll be okay, Reecy. I'll make sure they keep the plastic on everything."

That night was like no other I ever had. I had my mama, my girl, and my best friend all chilling up in the new house, and we didn't have a care in the world. The plasma TV was delivered along with a couple of new pieces that I bought at a furniture store. Later, that night when I went into the kitchen to get something to drink, Mom was standing looking around.

"So . . . you like it?"

"Boy, you know I do. I've always wanted one of these brownstones, ever since they started renovating them. See, these are nice, and they still are close enough to my people in The Vil. Thank you so much." Mom gave me a hug.

"Well, this is just the start of it because, after I get drafted, you're going to have a place there too."

"You sure you're not moving too fast, Langston? I don't want you to be like so many other athletes and entertainers who get some money then blow it. You have to be smart and build that money up and not just live rich."

"Yeah, I know. I got it covered. The real estate agent said this was a great investment."

"Good. Keep thinking businesslike. I like that."

"Since your ex sent me that note to watch my money, I have been all on it. I still don't like what he's into, but it was good that he looked out."

"He knows, Langston. I don't want you to think he has never cared about you. I have never told you that. He just wanted to do other things. I'm not faulting him anymore for anything we went through. It is what it is, almost like it was meant to be. We endured, and look, now my baby going to be a first-round pick."

Chapter Eighteen

Feedin' the Family

At this point, waiting was the hardest part. I couldn't even stand to watch *SportsCenter* or listen to sports on talk radio because everyone was speculating if my going pro overseas was going to spark some kind of mass rush for other high school players. There was also some talk that Barcelona would trade their pick for me if a team would offer them two first-round picks next year. I didn't think they would do it, but I knew it was business and didn't take it personal.

After being in the gym all morning, I went back to the new house for lunch, a nap then back out to do some cardio and weights. Mom was really feeling at home in her new place. I walked in the kitchen, and she and Tori were sitting at the breakfast bar.

I looked closer at Tori and noticed she was crying. "What's wrong?"

My mother touched Tori's hand then got up from the table and walked out.

I could spot some negative drama miles away, so I just took a deep breath and sat down next to Tori and waited for whatever was going on.

Tori didn't hesitate. "I'm pregnant," she pushed out with so much anger.

"Pregnant?"

"From the rape."

"What?"

"I missed my period, L, and I didn't think anything of it

because as soon as I got to the hospital after you found me, they gave me one of those morning-after pills. But those fools raped me for three days, three days and now, I'm pregnant."

Tori started bawling out of control. She had already been raped. Now she had to walk around knowing whatever happened to her was now inside of her.

My mother heard Tori crying and came back inside the kitchen and put her arm around her. I couldn't hang around this time. This was way too personal, even though she was my girl. I still needed to get out of there because I couldn't deal with hearing Tori cry and not being able to do a thing to make her stop. My body was on fire.

I went outside and started walking. Even though a lot of good things were happening, it didn't mean that the bad things that happened to Tori had been wiped away or were cool with me. I never complained to Tori because she had a lot to deal with, but she wasn't the same.

Jalen noticed it too. We knew we were going to give her some time, but we just didn't know how much she needed. The one and only time she tried to talk to me about what happened to her, I let her go as long as I could before telling her it was okay and that I couldn't take anymore. There was no way I wanted to hear about six or seven different fools taking turns with her for as long as they wanted no matter how much she begged them to let her go. Jalen told me that I should have gutted it out and listened, since she had to go through it, but I couldn't. Now, all of a sudden, she was pregnant.

When I stopped walking, I ended up on the exact corner where I tried slinging drugs when I was in the eighth grade. It only lasted for two days because my mother found out and put a stop to it, following me to school and back for months until she was sure I was back on track again.

Corners never change. It was still hard and dangerous with a bunch of dealers and users doing their thing to make money and get high. I stepped off the corner and across the street then looked back at the corner. Small kids were walking by, going into the nearby store to score some candy, but I knew that it was only a matter of time before they would be the ones on the corner selling the same drugs to a different generation.

I looked at all the houses boarded up at the doors and windows, and the little scuffles and disagreements happening over things that didn't really matter. It was depressing. All the drama on the street that day got to me, and right then and there was when I decided I wanted to build my first court and a recreation center for the kids, not just to learn how to play ball, but to learn about this life in the hood and how to make it better.

Some scrawny-ass dude brought me out of my glaze of what I was dreaming for the hood. He was wearing a baseball hat, worn-out white sneakers, torn jeans, and a tee.

"Yo', L, that package is nice. Thanks for thinking 'bout us!"

"Man, say what?"

"This package you got out on the street, it's straight up the truth, man," he said. "Smokers all over talking about how nice it is. Word on the street is, you pushing out on the big three—weed, coke, and the heroin. Like I say, good lookin'."

What he was saying was twisted in my mind. Before he got away from the block I had to holla back at him. "Yo', where you say you cop again?"

"I didn't, but one of your soldiers on Champion, right across from The Vil, hooked me up."

"Yeah, all right. But, listen, don't be putting my name on that package, you hear?"

The drug fiend looked back at me confused and smiled, showing the one rotten tooth left in his mouth, and walked away. "But we know it's you, L. It's smooth like you do on the court, baby. Yes, sir, it's you!"

Now I had two things pressing on my mind—Tori ,and

now a package on the street with my name attached. I started walking one way then stopped to walk in another. I was mad as hell and losing my mind. I wanted to get over on Champion to see who was putting my name on blast.

When I got there, my homie, Bed-Stuy, was standing on the corner like he was known to do. It looked to me like his business was booming. Me and Bed-Stuy were cool. He balled when we were on the court and had a nice game. Originally from Brooklyn, when his family moved into The Vil, he told us he went by Bed-Stuy, and we respected that. It seemed like everyone from New York could ball. A pure left-handed shooter, he made his name crossing ballers up and breaking ankles.

I walked over to him after he finished a transaction. Of course, we were both looking on the street for the police because I wasn't trying to get caught up.

"What up, Bed-Stuy?"

"Oh, snap! *L*, boogie up in here. What can I do for you, son?"

I paused, still looking out in the streets. "Need that info."

"On what? You been working out, *B*, getting ready for the pros, to show your shine or what?"

Two women who could have used some soap and water walked across the street and over to Bed-Stuy. He quickly brushed them away and pointed to one of his boys across the street who would give them what they needed.

"No doubt, I'm getting ready."

"So what you need out here on the block, *L*? This ain't no place for you to be hanging. Strays been flyin' with death on them, yo."

I looked around again at my surroundings. "Yo', my name on that package you moving?"

Bed-Stuy didn't answer back. He seemed uneasy, looking out in the street then back at me. He knew this was street business.

I pressed, "So?"

"Yeah, man. Got it last night, and selling like nothing before." Bed-Stuy gave me a quick glance then his eyes were back on the street.

"Who you wit' now?"

Bed-Stuy paused a long time. He took a few deep breaths. He wasn't trying to break the rules by giving up his supply. He stared me down a few seconds, moved his NY ball cap to the side of his head, and softened. "You goin' to make a brother proud when you turn pro, *L*."

"Bed-Stuy, when I cross a fool up with that move you taught me, I'm going to be sure to shout you out to the reporters."

He kind of smiled. "Oh, word?"

"Bond, baby."

"Murder One providing *L* package all day strong, and best believe, it's feeding the family. But you didn't hear it from me."

Chapter Nineteen
Money and Problems

I thanked Bed-Stuy for the information and stepped off the corner and around to the courts and hit Jalen on the cell. Out of all the people in the world to be blowing my name up on a package, it had to be Murder One. When I told J, he didn't seem surprised.

"I been meaning to tell you about that," Jalen said right before he smashed on the gas and pulled off down the street after picking me up.

"Tell me what?"

Jalen looked over at me then back at the road.

"Look, J, I ain't feeling no games today."

"Okay, look, man, I took a li'l bit of money I made with you and parlayed it on a package with Murder One."

"What?"

"It was like a good-faith deal, L."

"Fool, what are you talking about?"

Jalen smiled. I could see the excitement on his face.

"Murder One been seeing me floating the streets with the new wheels hard. They been hearing how people talking about how we coming up, and they stepped up and said they can triple some money if I was down."

"So you went into the drug business? Fool, have you lost your mind?"

"Naah, man. When you goin' to get it in your head, L? I'm a businessman. And if nobody else know that, you sure as hell should."

"J, you acting like you don't know?"

"Oh, I no."

"Man, do you know who you fucking with? Murder One do not play," I reminded him.

"They cool, man, all of them." Jalen nodded his head, trying to get me to agree with him.

I wasn't paying attention to where Jalen was driving, but he stopped in a back alley and got out of the car and started walking up to the backyard of an old house off Nelson Road.

"Wait a minute. Where you goin'?"

"Got to show you something, L. While you been in the gym working out, on my free time I been putting this together."

"Isn't this the house your aunt use to live in?"

"Now, you remember," Jalen said.

"I thought she was dead."

"She is. She gave this house to her sister. My aunt don't want it, so I'm using it." Jalen opened the door.

"Use it? Use it for what?"

Jalen looked around to make sure we weren't being watched. He led me into the house. We walked through the kitchen then the dining room then to the living room.

"It looks a little outta place right now, L, but check this out."

Jalen opened a door to a side room in the hallway, and inside there was a large room about the length of the house that had nothing but recording equipment inside, with about ten people inside putting things together, hooking up tables and cables.

"It's a little crazy right now, L, but you have just walked into J's playhouse, baby."

"Say what?"

"I'm starting a recording label." Jalen didn't give me a chance to look around or respond because he was out the room and leading me to the basement of the house. "And down here"—He pulled back some curtains after we were in the basement, and I couldn't believe my eyes. "It's my movie shop."

I had to squint my eyes to make sure what I was seeing was really happening. Three girls and a guy on a mattress were doing their freaky thing, while one guy held a camera and another held a long microphone under some huge lights. A member of Murder One was in the director's chair and watching the action go down.

I focused really close at one of the females on the mattress. I couldn't believe it was the nurse from the hospital that Jalen had met when we were trying to get in to see Tori.

Jalen looked up at me and smiled. "Pornos, baby. We already got twelve movies in the can. By this weekend, we going to have twelve more. Then we gonna package and wrap them up and get some ads out to *XXL* and *The Source* magazines, and we in bidness!" Jalen was all smiles and hit me on the arm. "*L*, who knew old girl from the hospital was such a freak?"

I grabbed Jalen by the back of his shirt and dragged him all the way up the stairs, through the kitchen and back outside to the back of the house, and stood him up as he yelled for me to let him go. "Fool, have you lost your mind?"

"*L*, get off me." Jalen tried to smooth out his gear and put his cap back on.

"What's your problem? Out here trying to be the don of the East side . . ."

"Man, so what? I'm just trying to double mine the best way I know how."

"By putting my name on a package?"

"That wasn't me. Murder One said they was going to try it, and when their product came back smashing and with your name ringing out at the same time, they twisted it together. It's that branding, *L*, that everybody is talking about. I read about it, and damn, it works like a mother."

"But I don't want my name branding on any drugs. And

you got girls in the basement freaking on video? What is your problem? You got to shut this down, J. We need to go to work on the things we talked about."

"I can't shut it down. Murder One came back with my money. I made stacks, L, and I'm letting it ride again on another two shipments."

"On my name?"

"L, look, what else we need to be doin' anyway?"

"I told your ass I wanted to put the courts up, do right on the streets. This here ain't going to work."

"I can't. Got too much invested to just throw it away."

"Jalen, you are not getting me fucked up with my contract, out here playing drug kingpin. You either drop this, take your losses, or we can't do this."

Jalen looked at me hard then back at the house. "L, people in the hood don't want no courts. They want money, weed, rap, and some women."

All I could do was stare Jalen in the eyes. It was plain as day that he had been overwhelmed by the quick money and had lost his mind off my success. During the last summer basketball camp I attended before my senior year, a few players in the league stood up and talked about, if you were lucky enough to make it as a pro, people that you know and love would start acting like your success was their own.

Jalen called me back the next day. He knew he had put my business in jeopardy and tried to make it right. He said he talked to Murder One about getting out of what they started, but they weren't hearing it. They told him the only way they wouldn't do business with him was if he came up with two million dollars cash. Murder One was a conglomerate of thugs who did business all over the city, just not the East side. They had the entire city on lock and had been doing it for years.

I remember when my mother told me about the police, in the same breath, she told me not to mess with Murder One. Their name explains it all. They would find themselves on trial for gruesome murders and never get convicted. Most people thought they even had the judges in the city bought off, but all I knew about them was to stay clear. But through association I was now connected.

I knew Murder One was playing Jalen, and they knew it too. It was what they did. They were trying to get into my pocket because he was my boy, but I wasn't going to let them faze me.

Murder One was Jalen's business, and I wanted no parts of it, and I was leaving it at that. They weren't getting any of my money.

Chapter Twenty

Your Turn

The first game of the NBA championship series had just ended, and Tori was asleep on my chest when my cell phone rang. It was Toy. He wanted to come by and pick me up so we could talk. I didn't want to be bothered, but it had been a rough day. I looked down at Tori's hand gently clutching her stomach and decided that getting away for a minute or two wasn't a bad idea.

Toy stopped and parked his car at The Strip Club.

"Man, they ain't going to let me up in here."

"That's where you're wrong. Your status carries privileges, if you didn't already know."

We went to the back door of the club that had VIP written on the door. Toy knocked twice, and a puffed-up bouncer who looked like he played for the Browns came to the door wearing a black shirt, do-rag, and shorts. He took one look at Toy and waved him in. He then looked up to me, nodded his head, then reached out to shake my hand.

It didn't take but a few seconds after we walked in before I began to feel like people were staring.

Toy found a table in the back. As we sat down, he smiled. "You comfortable? You all right?"

"I'm cool."

"Get used to the stares and looks. It's part of the lifestyle. You been in the newspaper every day for the last few weeks, so when people see a star they stare."

I could see the inside of the packed club through a large tinted window because VIP was sectioned off. I sat back and took it all in—at least four stages with the brass poles; females working them hard, while men made it rain, not to mention peeled eyes on the other side of the window looking at the ladies in thongs and no tops.

Toy yelled over the music, "First time, in a club?"

I nodded yes.

"Well, get used to this too. This is how the professional players relax . . . unless you going to stay in your room like a hermit and call girls in. But if you do, please don't catch a case."

"So what you want to talk about, Toy?"

"Look, Barcelona may deal you. They don't know. They like you, but they feeling if they can get two first-round picks later from a team, they will trade and wish you nothing but luck."

"Just business, man. I understand." I looked off into the club.

"You don't seem to be interested."

"It's cool, man. I just got a lot on my mind."

"Like what? I should know these things."

"My girl."

"And Jalen, I bet," he snuck in.

"How you know that?"

"That there's another reason why I wanted to bring you out to talk. Look, I know J's your boy, and I'm not spitting venom on him, but that knucklehead is running buck wild, and you need to check him. If you don't believe what I'm saying, I can take you in the streets and show you what I'm talking about."

"I know. I just found out about it, and I tried to talk to him."

"You did?"

"Yeah. He goin' to make it right."

"Drugs, skin flicks, a rap label with Murder One? What the hell is he thinking?"

"Money got to him. That's all I can think of."

"If I were you, I wouldn't have paid him until you left for overseas. Langston, you have to keep people who ain't never had nothing close to you. I don't care how much you love them. You can't let them out of your reach. Treat them like little kids."

By that time I knew Toy was right. Jalen was my boy, but anything he ever had was handed down to him after being recycled three or four times. But since we both were that way, I had to defend him a bit.

"Look, if he would have been talking all this he's doing before he got paid, I would have held out on him. But I should have kept my eyes open, 'cause Jalen has always been about doubling his up."

"How much you line his pockets with?" Toy asked.

"A hundred seventy gees."

Toy's eyes bugged out. "Gotdamn! He can do a lot of damage on the streets with that."

"Already has. Got my name on a package running the entire East side."

Toy was scanning the club. "And I hear they're making money hand over fist too."

"You heard my name on the package, Toy?"

"L, look at me. The streets know me. We friendly like that."

"Man, I don't need this right now."

"That's why you gotta let him go. Cut him off."

"I already told him to close shop."

"That ain't what I'm talking about."

"What you mean?"

Toy pushed up his chair closer to the table to make sure I was the only one who could hear him. "Exactly what I said. Let him go. Make sure people in the hood know he ain't riding with you anymore."

"Man, ain't nobody ever going to believe that. Me and Jalen been hanging since we been on tricycles."

"Yeah, and he still acting like a three-year-old who found a Blow Pop on the sidewalk next to the candy shop. He has put our shit in jeopardy. Don't you get what I'm telling you?"

I still wasn't comfortable with Toy coming across like we were partners by mutual choice.

"I know that look, *L*."

"What you mean?"

"You think, 'cause I got some baggage, I can't get right. Let me tell you something. Just by landing you has had my phone ringing off the hook from kids who have heard from somebody that they should go pro overseas just like you. But guess what?"

"What's that?"

"They have a better chance of hitting the lottery than seeing that dream come true. You right now have the chance to do real big things, and it's a shame you don't see the big picture yet. The only reason you don't see it is because no one has schooled you on all the possibilities, except for Coach Pierce, who is as old-school as they come, and your mother, who, with all due respect, doesn't know a damn thing about basketball and what this can do for you on a global level. Now, if your dad was in the picture, it would be different 'cause I know he knows business, but he ain't involved. You know what I mean?"

I sort of laughed Toy off.

"Don't diss me, *L*. I'm trying to get you to understand."

"Back off, Toy. I'm listening."

"How do you think I got your deal with the shoe company in the first place? You think they just saw you in a magazine and said, 'He's the one we want'?"

Toy had my attention, because I had wondered how it all came about.

"Well, that's not how it happened. I pitched you to them. Told them you were from the life of every young black boy's dream who come out the hood. Don't get me wrong. You got other young bucks out in them suburbs who dream about the league too, but guess what, *L?* That ain't their only dream or possibility. Them marketing cats at New Funk wanted you 'cause I got in their heads and let them know that you were the truth, of everything going on in the ghetto."

"The truth, huh?"

"Gotdamn right! Tell me something. How many ballers from the hood make it to the pros?"

"I don't know, Toy."

"I know you don't. It's only twelve active on the roster at one time that play that eighty-one-game schedule. So out of those twelve, on the thirty teams, how many of them slots you think the owners going to let some ghetto-ass, grit-eating negro, who grew up in the projects pasting posters of Magic, Jordan, and Iverson on them cinderblock concrete walls we both know so much about have?"

"I don't know, Toy, but I know you're going to tell me."

"I don't know either, but I tell you this. It's only three or four pure ghetto ballers who know what it feels like to hear their stomachs grumbling strong for two, three days at a time who are in the league. If there were more, New Funk would have already had a soldier in the league to rock their gear. You feel me?" Toy took a deep breath, looked over the club, then back at me. "Look, man, all I'm trying to say is, you're truly what the players in the league are trying to mimic. And once you get your ass in there after two years overseas, you're going to have to be strong. Understand what I'm saying. Look through all the cornrows you see, way past the humongous Afros, tattoos, hard looks, and snarls you get. Them players putting on forays, Langston. They ain't harder than the softest fool you done walked past every day in the hood on your way to school. I done played with most of them, and they ain't doing nothing but filling a void created by the hood and hip-hop music then expanded to the league. Why you think they have a dress code now? Better yet, how come none of them so-called, roughnecks have put their foot down and said, 'To hell with the dress code. I've been dressing hard all my life?' 'Cause they frontin'. You see what I'm sayin'? Gettin' paid off trends from the hood. New Funk knows that. You're going to be representing every black kid from the hood who thinks his only shot of being somebody is playing ball." Toy got up from the table and walked away to the bar to talk to someone he knew.

He must have had me twisted though. Even though I did agree with some of the things he said, he had to know about the hood and the love between me and Jalen. I knew Jalen was out there rolling with a big smile on his face because he had new money, but he was the one person I knew had my back, whether he was doing right or wrong.

Earlier that night for some reason I thought back to the time Jalen stepped up to a guy twice his size with a pistol and told him to back up off me because he was willing to die for me. That was the hood love I knew I had with Jalen. I decided right then and there, no matter how Toy felt about it, I was going to call my boy up later that night to tell him to stop his madness and get ready to get down to business, so we could get away from the hood.

My thoughts must have really been deep because I barely paid any attention to the lights when they were dimmed even lower than they already were, and the topless girl in a thong sat down next to me with a mask covering her face. She licked her lips a few times. "You having a good time?" she whispered.

"It's cool," I told her. "Just chilling. Sort of like on business."

"Oh, we all on business, baby. Believe that. You ain't never been up in here before, have you?"

"Naah, not really."

"Oh, I know who you are. You're that ballplayer 'bout to go pro."

I didn't like getting recognized so easily. It made me feel

like everyone who looked at me wanted something. I nodded my head yes to her.

I didn't ask her to, but she straddled my lap. Then she looked around at the other girls in the room who had come in with her who were already dancing for guys sitting up in VIP. She told me to relax and enjoy her show.

She didn't have to move but once or twice after she climbed up into my lap before I realized she had me excited, so I just went with the flow.

Everyone was enjoying themselves, including Toy, who sat on a stool at the bar getting his.

The dancer was working it so hard on my lap, I was beginning to wonder if she taught Ciara how to work it. She started nibbling on my neck then my ear. Then she asked if I wanted to walk with her to a room downstairs.

At first I told her no, but she kept kissing my neck, like she knew it was my spot, and she made me change my mind. I lifted her off my lap and stood her on the ground.

She grabbed my hand and pulled me down to whisper in my ear. Then she pulled off her mask. "Told you I'd get you back."

It was Katrina.

Chapter Twenty-one

Handling Mine

I was sleeping like a baby until I heard, "*L*, wake up. It's almost twelve."

All the pushing and nudging, combined with my hang-over, made me want to scream out.

"*L*, you have to wake up. You have to get out of here."

I pushed my eyes open.

Tori just kept talking. "I thought you had something to do?"

My head was under a pillow, so the guilt from being with Katrina didn't hit me until Tori ripped the covers off me and I saw her face.

"Don't you have some place to be? That court thing or something?"

"I do?" I really couldn't remember.

"And don't forget about your interview with *Sports Illustrated*. I think you said they were calling around four."

"What time is it?"

"I told you almost twelve. Dang! You are so out of it. Where did Toy take you last night?"

"The Strip Club."

Tori echoed me. "The Strip Club?"

"Mmm-hmm." I felt myself dozing back off.

"Stop lying, Langston. You know you weren't up in no stank strip club."

"If you say so."

I felt Tori plop her little one-hundred-twenty-pound self on the bed. "Why? Why did you go there?"

"I didn't go. Toy took me."

"I know that much, fool. But for what?"

"I guess that's where he hangs out to talk business."

"Business?"

"Yeah, he was trying to tell me about how all the black kids in every ghetto and hood in America going to be looking up to me."

"Oh, word?"

"Yeah, and the main reason I got the shoe deal was because I'm the product of the hood and I don't have to front about knowing the streets, like a lot of players do."

Tori was silent for a moment. "So you see anything you like in there?"

"Naah."

By this time I was out of the bed and in the bathroom, dumping mouthwash into my mouth.

"C'mon, you can tell me."

I got rid of the mouthwash in the sink. "Everyone looked the same to me."

Tori folded her arms. "Well, you know it's okay if you want to see other females right now."

"Why would I want to do that?"

"'Cause you should. You know my mother doesn't want me to get an abortion. She told me she doesn't know if it's right, and if I wanted to have the baby, she would take care of it, while we live our lives."

"Your mother said that?"

"Yes, but my sisters think I should go down to the clinic as soon as possible and have the abortion."

I was speechless. I never formed an opinion on abortion. The whole thing about the situation was almost too much for me. It really was just too damn early to even discuss.

"What's wrong, *L*?"

"Nothing."

"Has to be something. All of a sudden you changed and got quiet on me."

"Just thinking about all this stuff Toy was talking about last night."

"'Bout me?"

"No. About how things are because I'm going pro. Tori, you know that if I wasn't going pro and this shit happened to you, I would kill somebody, right?"

"I know, L. Don't say it, okay."

"And it pisses me off 'cause the police ain't doing nothing about it. They act like what happened to you don't even matter. I'm just saying, going pro is kind of like turning me into some kind of punk or something 'cause I can't even begin to reach out and find who did this to you. I just want some 'get-back.' "

"That's not true, L. You ain't nobody's punk. This is turning you into a man. Everybody can see it."

Nothing Tori could say was going to change my mind about how I felt. It just seemed like get-back was in my blood just as much as anything else. It was a part of me and something I knew I was never going to let go of.

Tori said, "So, you thought about what I should do?"

"About what?"

She tapped on her stomach, making me a little queasy.

"No. I mean, not really. It's your choice."

"But if I have this baby, it would never know its father."

I was blunt. "How many of us know that anyway?"

"So you think I should have it?"

"I'm just saying, Do you think it's reason enough to just kill the baby 'cause you don't know who the father is?"

"I don't know," she said. "I don't."

Chapter Twenty-two
Just like That

I met with the construction crew I chose to build the new court in the hood, a group of men I had seen for the longest around the way who did a lot of work on the homes on the East side. They let me know they could get the court up and running in no time. They were surprised that I picked a black crew to do a project because most of the projects that really mattered went to the white-owned crews who drove in from the North side.

We decided to sit down and talk about the plans for the recreation center after the court was finished. I had planned for Jalen to organize it all, since that was his thing, but I hadn't seen him since he dragged me out to his money-making operation. And I didn't get to call him the night before like I planned because of the time I spent with Katrina. Surprisingly, after I talked with the crew, Jalen pulled up.

Jalen looked around while we stood on the spot. "So this is where you going to put the court up?"

"Yeah, right here. You like?"

"Which way the court running?"

I moved my arm up and down.

"Naah, man, the sun going to be eating them up that way. Look, you gotta go this way with it. See, no sun."

"A'ight, a'ight. You right."

Jalen was looking good, geared up from head to toe, and it looked like he had on a new wrist watch.

"You like the watch, *L*? I see you peeping game."

"Fool, shut up, and forget the watch. I'm out here worrying about this, when you should be handling it for me, instead of flossing all through the streets. I can't be out here worrying about what direction the court needs to go in. Damn!"

"Look, man—"

"No, hold up, J. We made a deal. We been working on this thing for years. Don't you think every time I had practice and didn't want to go, going pro and having you, supposedly my boy, at my side was on my mind, so I went? All the times I have taxed my body out to go pro, all of that wasn't for me. It was for your little black ass too!"

"But you said—"

"I know what I said, and I'm telling you now you need to get back with this 'cause this right here is real, and I can't handle all these details by myself."

Jalen tugged on his jean jacket and looked at his Escalade. He understood what I was saying but just had to let me know. "What I'm doing is real too, B."

"Yeah, it's real, but you wouldn't be doing any of it if it wasn't coming from what I do. Now, that's real."

Jalen pulled his arm up to check his watch. "Yeah, yeah, you right. But I got business deals going. Murder One ain't going to let me out, and our deal is almost done. After this last package and the movies wrap up—Oh, L, you should see—"

"I don't want to see it, J. All I want to do is get my camp together and get ready to play ball."

"You going to be ready, man. Don't worry."

"All this stuff I need to do, Jalen."

"So what Toy doing?"

"Toy is Toy, man. He thinks I need to leave you alone though."

"He said that?"

"Yeah, he thinks you're messing up things for him too. I told you, Jalen, this street shit and the corporate board room don't mix."

"A'ight, a'ight. Look, I'm goin' to do better."

"When, Jalen? Overseas draft coming up, people calling for interviews, this court needs to be up before I leave, and we need someplace to live as soon as I find out where I will be for sure. You expect me, to handle all that?"

Jalen looked around. "I'm leaving all this alone. I'll get things rolling by next week." He flung his hands like it was a done deal.

"Naah, man, today. You start today."

"Doing what?"

"I need to work out, and I need someone to get this court situated. C'mon, I'll tell you everything while you drop me past the house to get my workout gear. You got your gear in the car? You ready to work out too?"

"I stay ready," Jalen insisted.

It had been raining all morning, so the streets were still wet. Jalen plopped down the traction on the Escalade. We were zooming right past The Vil when we noticed about thirty people standing in a circle. Nobody had to tell us there was a fight going down.

Jalen parked the Escalade, and the circle just opened up for us as we got closer to see what was going on. It was Tori and Katrina pushing and arguing, about to go to blows.

I stepped in to break them up and a few ol'-school heads, a bunch of horny old bastards who wanted to see them rip each other's clothes off, begged me to let them fight.

Katrina's lip was bleeding, and Tori's shirt was torn a few inches.

"You better control this bitch, L!" Katrina shouted. "Or she gonna find herself picking that ass up off the pavement!"

"You need to go take care of that lip before I bust the other one, skank," Tori told her.

"Hold up, hold up! What's this all about?" I tried to find out.

Katrina said, "She just mad because I was with you last night, and I'm going shoppin' with the money you gave me."

Jalen swiped his face and put his head up toward the sky then mumbled, "And he talking about I'm the one messing up."

So now I was getting mad and trying to hush Katrina's mouth because she was putting me on blast.

"Is that true, *L*? You were with her last night, while I was sleeping in your bed waiting for you?"

I heard a few moans from those standing in the circle. Some called me a player, others were saying how dirty I was to treat Tori that way.

"Look, it wasn't even like that, Tori," I tried to tell her.

"Well, how was it then?" Katrina pushed.

"*L*, I thought you loved me?" Tori cried out.

"How could he love yo' ass, when he was with me?"

My head was going back and forth listening to their bull, and I didn't know how to get in the conversation or make them stop going at each other. "Are y'all going to let me say anything about this?"

"I don't have no beef with you, baby," Katrina said. "It's this bitch that I don't like."

"C'mon, Katrina," I said to her.

"You the only bitch out here!" Like lightning, Tori reached around and smacked the taste out of Katrina's mouth, and everyone in the crowd sounded as though they felt the sting when it landed.

I held them away from one another. "Look, y'all need to cut this out!"

"Were you with her last night, *L*?"

I couldn't believe Tori blew up the spot. If I'd told her no, she would have known I was lying just by the look on my face, so I didn't say a word. She turned around and ran off.

I turned around and looked at Jalen, who was getting his chance to look at me and make me feel bad for my decision and what I had going on.

Katrina moved in on me. "So what we goin' to do tonight, baby?"

"We ain't doin' nothing," I told her. "Out here runnin' your mouth."

"Oh, it's like that?"

I nodded yes while I watched Tori walk away. That's when Katrina tried to smack me, but right before her hand reached my face, I grabbed it. She kept trying to reach at my face, so I pushed her hand back a bit, and she screamed out in pain.

All of a sudden, a few guys stepped up, one of whom was her cousin.

"Yo', I don't give a fuck who you are. You ain't goin' to be touching her like that." The guy talking was about six feet tall, dark-skinned, and had a gold tooth in the front.

When they started to walk up on me, Jalen lifted up his shirt and took out a pistol, and people started scurrying and running, some tripping, to get out the way.

Even after all that happened, a few people walked up to me and wished me good luck overseas. As we walked away from the beef and back to the car, it was starting to rain, more like a mist.

For some reason, Jalen had gotten a charge from what just went down. "You see that, *L*?"

"I saw it. Where'd you get that tool from?"

"Streets. Never know when you goin' to need it, right? People out here acting brand-new, like they can't catch no lead. Have they forgotten this The Vil?"

"This is crazy, man. Let's get Tori."

We were about two steps from getting in the car when Toy showed up and pulled his wheels in front of us and got out and slammed his car door shut. "So that's how we doin' it now?" he said, his arms wide open.

Jalen looked at me then back at Toy.

"Look, man, who could have expected that to happen?" I told him.

"That's what I'm trying to tell you, L. You have to expect it now. Being challenged is part of this new life I was telling you about. And what you don't need is some scrawny, tilted-Kangol punk throwing a gun in somebody's face every time you get into a situation."

"Who's this guy again?" Jalen asked. "Is he your agent or your daddy? I ain't been gone but a couple of days, so you need to fill a brother in on his status."

Toy pointed at Jalen hard. "Shut up, boy! Shut up before I hurt you." He started walking toward Jalen.

Jalen took one step backward then lifted up his shirt, showing him his steel.

"Oh, it's like that?"

"It's just like that," Jalen let him know. "I am not playing today, Toy."

Chapter Twenty-three

Come and Talk to Me

I probably called Tori's name ten times before she finally looked back at me and Jalen creeping behind her as she walked down the street, trying to cover her head from the mist.

"Leave me alone, L."

I was stretched out the window. "What do you mean, leave you alone? C'mon, get in the car with us. We're going to work out then go get something good to eat."

"Do it by your damn self." Tori stopped walking and put her hands on her hips.

Jalen stopped. "No, no. Go get yo' ho to go with you. She gotta be hungry from last night anyway."

Tori started walking away again. She was good at rubbing things in when she was mad at me, but I had to let what she was giving bounce off me because I wanted to at least try to explain.

We continued to follow her.

"Are you going to let me tell you what happened or what?"

She shouted back, "I already know! You and Katrina was knocking boots last night, just like she said. You embarrassed me, L."

There was nothing I could say back to Tori because I knew it was true. Tori wasn't the type to play like she was married or about to be when she was in high school, but when I told her that I wanted to marry her, the game changed. She took being with me more serious than I did.

"Get out, *L*," Jalen pushed. "Go talk to her, with your cheating ass."

I looked over at Jalen. "Man, forget you with that! Just stop. Stop."

Jalen slammed on the brakes. I don't know if he was trying to make me hit my head on the dash or not, but his hard stop didn't work because I put my hand out and braced myself. I looked at him hard before I got out. "Bitch-ass!"

"Cheater," he said back.

"Just wait here."

"You better go out there and beg."

I ran to catch up with Tori. "Tori, wait a minute."

"No, *L*. I'm going home. I'll have somebody come by and get my stuff."

"Hold up, hold up. Why do you have to go there? Look, I made a mistake, but it wasn't my fault."

Tori stopped and looked at me. "Not your fault?"

"Naah, not really. Look . . ."

Tori took off walking again, so I grabbed her arm.

She stopped and looked at my hand. "Get off me!"

"Are you going to talk to me or what?"

"I said get off me!"

I let go and was surprised she didn't start walking again. I thought that was my chance.

"Okay, look, I messed up. Toy took me to the club. He left me at a table by myself, and all these dancers came inside and they had on masks. I didn't even know Katrina worked there. She was butt naked up in that piece, shaking it, and she came over to me. It was dark, and one thing led to another. That's what happened."

Tori stared at me. "I don't care anymore, okay." She started to walk away again.

"You don't care? You don't care about what?"

"I don't care about this. I don't care about you sleeping with that nasty slut or us being together either."

"C'mon, you're just saying that."

"No, I mean it. I have too much to worry about. Have you forgotten about this baby inside of me? Have you forgotten I just got raped by a bunch of fools who could have gave me more than just this baby to worry about? I just don't care anymore, L, so you and Jalen go to wherever you guys end up and have a good life."

"I'm not going anywhere without you."

"Why do you want me to go with you so bad? I mean, really, what is the deal? Because if you think I'm going to be like all those wives of pro players who play dumb to what their men are doing, for the perks, you got me twisted."

"You know that ain't the reason, Tori."

"Well, what's the reason? Is it because you feel sorry for me? You feel sorry that I was raped and left for dead? You're sorry that I was saving myself and had it all taken away? Is that what it is?"

By now Tori was crying uncontrollably. I would have never imagined us having this conversation, but we were, and it wasn't a good time.

"Tori, you know I love you. Let's just forget about this. If you want me to stay home every night, I will. I mean, I don't care anymore. Everything else is not even worth it."

Tori looked up at me, and with all that she was going through, she kind of smiled. "I can't, L. I don't trust you now." Then she ran down the street away from me and didn't stop when I called out to her.

Chapter Twenty-four

The Game

I started walking after her.

"*L*, just let her go for now," Jalen called out. "You need to work out."

I took my time getting back into the front seat.

"Did I hear Tori say she was pregnant? Tell me I didn't hear that."

"You heard. She said it, *J*."

Jalen gave me a weird look.

"From the rape, man, not me."

Jalen was quiet for a few blocks. "Whew! From the rape? Damn!"

"Yeah. She told me a few days ago."

We got to the gym, but Jalen didn't help much, spending most of his time on the bench, probably thinking about Tori. No doubt, she was his sister that nobody could mess with.

About two hours later, Toy met up with us. We still had to eat, so. He was throwing out different types of investments that he thought would make the seventeen million grow, especially the abandoned downtown real estate that was in good-enough shape to make lofts.

"This is with respect, Toy, but I don't like any of these ideas," Jalen said. "People barely making ends meet, and they not really looking to move."

"Oh, so you don't like what I got on the table?"

"Sure don't," Jalen told him. "People broke. Who goin' to buy?"

"Well, what would you rather L do? Drop a few million in your chick-flick hookup?"

"You've been all up in mine, haven't you?"

"You should never think I don't know what's going on in the streets, Jalen."

Jalen laughed Toy off. "I just think L should sit on his money. Get interest off it and wait to see what the contract from his new team is going to be. Then play the first season and half of the second, before he goes to the NBA and then look at things."

Toy took quick offense to Jalen and looked around be-fore he spoke. "Look, L, your partner here is stunting your growth. The only way to make money is to put your money in investments that will work. I mean, look what he did. Got paid, went into the streets, and got paid again. You got paid on your investment, didn't you, Jalen?"

"Yeah, I got paid. But that's me, not L. He got more money than I will ever see. I took what I got and topped off on it. That's how we do. I done tripled mine, and now I'm out and I'm happy with that. Just like Biggie used to say when we was growing up, 'No car note or payment, I'm down with that.'"

"I'm kind of feeling Jalen on this, Toy. I mean, there's no rush to making these deals. Those buildings downtown been vacant for years, so I don't see no rush on that."

Jalen pointed at me with his chicken wing. "Exactly."

Toy smiled at Jalen. "You know, for you to never done anything, you sure know a lot about everything."

"Yeah, like the fact you didn't even get drafted after you told everyone you were going in the first round."

"You sure that's how it went down?" Toy asked Jalen.

"Didn't see your name on the draft board and to think they had way more than two rounds in the draft back in the day."

"Oh, I see you think you're a baller yourself?"

"I gets mine. Believe that," Jalen said.

Toy looked at me then smiled. "Is that right?"

"No doubt. My crossover would probably break those dusty, brittle ankles." Jalen laughed.

"You care to make a wager on it?"

"All you gotta do is say when and where?"

"Okay, one on one. If I lose, I'll tear up my contract with L. If I win, you step off."

"Where we playin'?"

"Midnight, under the lights in The Vil."

"Damn! It takes you that long to digest that food, old man?"

No matter how I tried to get Toy and Jalen to just chill about the matter, they weren't hearing it. Toy said Jalen needed to respect him, and Jalen told me, once and for all, he was going to get Toy up from under what we always dreamed about doing together.

I hung around the house trying to get Tori on the phone for a few hours, but she wouldn't answer.

Twelve o'clock rolled around, and we were at the courts. I smashed on the lights.

"Look at this, L," Jalen said. "Your boy ain't even showing up with his sorry, washed-up self." Jalen took an eighteen-footer from the right elbow. "Pow! See, that's what I'm talking about. He didn't want this."

Out of the darkness from the side of one of the buildings, Toy came out and walked onto the court. "You know you're not getting that off on me, don't you? You need to go ahead and take a few more shots 'cause any shot you take soon after going right back in your face."

Jalen nodded at Toy. "Hey, man, what kind of sneakers you got on?"

Toy looked down.

"Them jones been outta style at least ten years!" Jalen yelled at the top of his voice, knowing it was going to echo through The Vil. "Oh my goodness, y'all, Toy got on some 'bo-bo's.'"

"Don't matter what I'm wearing. Besides, I'm just wait-ing til' my New Funks arrive. Ain't that right, L?"

I bounced the ball a few times then went up for a soft dunk. "Y'all need to chill, man. Let's just play some ball out here. Forget about the one-on-one."

"No, no, he wants to play," Toy said. "He wants to play for our relationship with you, L. If he wins, I quit, I'm gone, ghost. But if I win, this young thundercat is back in the porn business. Hell, he might have to star in a couple of movies him-self. Call himself Wesley Pipes or something."

"A'ight, if y'all goin to play, play then."

Toy had his hands extended and ready to receive the ball. "My ball out," he said. "Eleven–straight."

"Your ball out? You must be high. Shoot for it," Jalen told him.

"Let L shoot for it. He make it, I got it. He miss, your ball."

"From the corner though," Jalen said.

I ran over to the corner. "Oh, you don't think I'm good from here, J?"

"I know you, L," Jalen said.

I missed, and Toy looked at me. "I know you missed that on purpose, L," he said, pissed.

Jalen took the ball and threw it to Toy. "Check, old man."

"Oh, I got your old man." Toy threw the ball back.

Jalen said, "Here, check it again. Got enough air for you?"

Toy just threw the ball back at Jalen and moved in closer to him.

Jalen sat the ball back down and walked away from it. "Check it again, damn it! I don't want it to be no mistake after I wax this ass."

"Baby girl, you going to play ball or not?" Toy asked, getting more agitated.

Jalen was still about five steps from the ball. "You sure you ready? 'Cause, when I pick it up, you're not touching it again."

Toy got down in his defensive position and looked at Jalen.

"I guess that means yes." Jalen ran up, picked up the ball, stood for a few seconds then blew past Toy for a layup.

I knew *J* was going to do that. He always tried that on me. That's why I never played up close on him. He was too quick to try and stay up on.

Jalen took the ball back again. "Check," he said.

"Don't give me no more damn checks."

"You hear that, *L*? No more checks, he said."

"Shut up and play, Jalen," I told him.

Jalen took the ball and blew past Toy again for another layup. "I told you, old man. You goin' to need some checks because, I don't care what you did in the past, now is now. and right now, I'm busting that ass."

By the time Toy finally got the ball from Jalen, he was losing five to zip.

"You should have kept going to the bucket instead of shooting that tired jumper," Toy told him.

"That's okay. I won't miss again."

But that was it for Jalen. I couldn't believe it. Toy hit eleven straight jumpers all from twelve to eighteen feet. In Jalen's face.

After the last shot went in, Toy ran up under the basket, picked up Jalen's ball, and threw it clear across to the other end of the court. "Now, take your ass on!" he shouted out loud.

"Man, forget that! If you think I'm out, you must be smoking."

"Look, we had a bet. You're out."

Jalen and Toy looked at me.

"You did bet, J."

"L, you don't bet no job, you don't bet your paycheck."

Toy said, "You sure as hell did."

"I told you, J. You just too reckless, man. Now you got yourself messed up for betting."

"L?"

"Serious, man. You lost."

Jalen looked at Toy, the rim, the court, then back at me. "You serious, man?"

"Hey, you're the one who made the bet."

"Man, forget y'all! Good luck with your tore-up abandoned buildings. I hope that shit fall down the first day you buy it, L."

Jalen began to walk away, and he was almost all the way off the court when the lights were switched off.

"Lights out for your ass, Jalen. I mean, Wesley Pipes or whatever your name is. Let's go to the club, L."

I stood as Jalen walked away then called out to him.

He stopped. "What?"

"C'mon back, fam."

"What is this?" Toy wanted to know.

"You not out, man, but stop running your mouth so much, 'cause now you see what can happen."

"Nah, nah, L. I won, so he's gone."

"Look, Toy, I'm the only one around here who loses his job shooting the rock, not you or Jalen."

Toy looked at me hard. "Yeah, all right, all right."

Chapter Twenty-five
Why like This?

"For someone who is about to be drafted in the European draft, you don't seem too happy. I hope you don't look that way when all the cameras are in your face when they call your name." My mother was looking down at me while I was stretched out on our new leather couch.

"Do I look that bad?"

"Yup, you look like you done pissed your fiancée off because you messed with some trifling skank on the hush."

"Ma, how you sound?"

"Like a concerned mother. How many times do I have to tell you, if you going to be with one girl, you have to be with her all the way 'cause when you don't, it brings nothing but drama."

"It wouldn't be any drama if she just stayed with the program."

"Who are you talking about?"

"Tori."

"Boy, you sound like one of these wannabe pimps walking around on Mt. Vernon who got their game from BET or something. If you haven't forgotten, Tori was raped. Any other time she might have forgave you, like all the other times."

"What?"

"Don't you dare try to play me. Tori tells me everything. If you ask me, you're being selfish, running off with that girl."

"Can't I make a mistake without all the drama?"

"Drama? This is more than drama. Tori loves you. What if she went out one night, slept with a guy one or two times just because he was there? What would you think about it?"

"She wouldn't do that though."

"You must be out of your mind, boy."

"What? She wouldn't."

"Okay, L, if you think women don't just because they say they are committed to you and love, you're going to get turned out."

"Tori wouldn't do it, 'cause I know her."

"I see you have your mind set on her being so faithful to you. Unbelievable. But just remember one thing, mister man. Women do as much damage as men. And if you let one tell you she's not, not saying Tori is, because I like her, you have another think coming, if you think women don't step out."

"Well, I didn't mean for this to happen. It was a mistake, and we have to move on."

"From what she told me, you embarrassed her."

"You talked to Tori?"

My mother smiled. "Yes. Why?"

"About what? When?"

"We talked a few times, and it's none of your business what we talked about. But I'll tell you this. All you should be worried about is this draft coming up and where you will be playing ball. Everything else will work out on its own."

"You sure about that?"

"Boy, are you questioning me?"

So I took my mother's advice and tried to think about leaving and playing ball overseas. It seemed strange going into the supermarket and buying a basketball magazine instead of stealing it. I was also tripping on how all the writers and so-called experts were saying I would go overseas and that my decision would change the NBA draft forever.

Jalen was with me, and we jumped in his ride when we came out of the store.

"Where to?" he asked.

"I don't care, man. Let's just cruise. I can't take sitting in the house any longer. This draft can't even come fast enough."

"We need to get our suits for draft day anyway," Jalen said.

"I ain't wearin' no suit, man."

"Oh yes, you are. They're going to have all kinds of coverage down here, since we not flying over. You better get ready to play the part. I know I am."

"Yeah, okay, but Max better have hooked it up just like he did for graduation."

"L, you know how he do it. He's been keeping players nice on the East side since we were pups."

"On the real though . . . if Tori was rolling with us, this would be the time of our lives."

"Man, Tori wants to be there."

"How you know?"

"She told me."

"When?"

"Last night."

"Damn! She talkin' to everybody but me. What she say?"

"Told me she wanted to be there for you, but she wasn't going out like that, L. I can't believe you got with Katrina again. You let her mess up our dream."

"How was I supposed to know she was going to run her mouth?"

"Man, from now on, you might as well realize that any female you hit, they goin' to run they mouth. That's why so many pro players aren't married. They ain't trying to be held to no unrealistic odds."

"What you mean by that?"

"Ladies everywhere, temptation, big boobs, big butts, pretty faces all ripe for the picking. Act like you know."

"So you don't think I should marry Tori?"

"Yeah, if she'll marry you back and you act right. If not, don't do it."

"It's just hard to talk to her now. When I try to get close, she backs up, and then I have to think about every single word I say to her. It's not easy. And it ain't like I haven't been trying to work with her. What happened to her was so foul, man, and it's messed us up."

"Well, I'm not getting in yo' business, but she know you've been trying."

"How?"

"'Cause I told her when I was trying to talk her into hanging out with us during the draft."

"You think she'd come if I ask her?"

Jalen shook his head no.

"Why not?"

"Told me she want you to know that you messed up, and if she's not there, you're going to know how it feels when she isn't there for you."

"Oh, it's like that?"

"That's the way it be."

While we were driving, Jalen slowed down on the street and tried to look down a side street but couldn't see like he wanted to. So he began to look for a spot where he could turn around and go back.

"What's wrong?"

"Toy . . . I think I saw his wheels."

"Naah, couldn't be. Keep moving. He's at the crib waiting on a fax from the public relations chick who is supposed to set up a trip overseas when I find out what's going on."

Jalen didn't answer me. He did a U-turn, put on his left blinker, and waited for a few cars to pass before he turned.

Sure enough, it was Toy parked on the curb. Jalen didn't pull up right behind him. He parked far enough away where we had to get out the car. He walked in front of me and looked in from the passenger side.

I stopped and looked around, wondering where Toy could have been.

Jalen knocked on the window. "Oh, L, you gotta see this," he said.

I took a few steps closer and stopped when I saw her head lift up from his lap and turn toward the window. Through the dark tint on the window, I could tell it was Katrina.

Toy looked over at us then got out. "What y'all doin' out here?"

"I guess we don't have to ask you the same question," Jalen said. "Out here getting some."

Toy told Jalen to shut up and he tried as best as he could to get his clothes together.

I looked in the car to get a better look at Katrina, who had no shame to her game. I quickly began to understand what my mother was saying about some of the ladies running around crazy, doing whatever to whoever. At that moment, I promised myself I would never touch her again. There was no telling how many others she was getting with.

"So you get that fax, Toy?" It was the only question I could think of asking him.

"Yeah, it came through 'bout an hour ago," he said. "I was going to call you later."

All of a sudden Katrina got out the car. "How long you going to be, Toy?" she asked, her hands on her hips.

"Look, I got business to take care of, so it looks like you walking from here."

"Oh, hell no. I ain't walking nowhere. You brought me over here, and you taking me back."

Toy was done smoothing out his clothes then walked over to Katrina. "Bitch, what I tell you?"

"I said I ain't walking, Toy," she said back.

Without hesitation, Toy smacked Katrina, knocking her to her knees, and she starting crying.

"Naah, Toy, that's not right." Jalen walked over to Katrina and helped her up.

"Yo', Toy, what's your problem?" I asked him.

"Look, *L*, forget her. She ain't nothing but a tramp, a'ight. You know it, I know it, and if Jalen keep being nice to her, he goin' to know it too."

Jalen started walking Katrina away. "C'mon, I'll take you home," he said. "Fuck him!"

"Fuck me?" Toy yelled. "You talking to me?" He edged toward Jalen.

Jalen stopped and turned around. I thought he was going to pull up his shirt again and flash his tool, as did Toy, because he hesitated and his eyes widened.

"You heard me, Toy. You ain't right, hitting her like that. She ain't deserve that."

"Just take the bitch home," Toy said. "Katrina, I will get with you later."

Katrina was still crying and holding her face. "Forget you!"

Toy put a fake smile on his face. "Look, *L*, I'm going to the crib. I'll call you when I get there, so we can talk about the fax."

I didn't even answer Toy. I just watched him try to laugh the situation off. Then he got in his ride and took off.

Chapter Twenty-six
I Got That

We decided on the spur of the moment to go to New York City for the draft, instead of staying in Columbus. Jalen really wanted to go overseas to check everything out, but we didn't even have passports yet, which took some time to get. I decided to go to New York, so I could let my mom shop. Plus, as the media mecca, Toy wanted us to line up interviews there, since my jump to overseas would be monumental and more than likely lead the way for future high school ballers to do the same.

While on the plane, I knew my life would never be the same again after I returned to Columbus. I would officially be a professional basketball player. Everything I had ever dreamed of was about to come true. We flew first-class, and Jalen was up in there like he had lost his mind, ordering food he knew he wasn't going to eat and tripping out when the flight attendant gave us all steaming-hot cloths.

Jalen placed his over his face and asked for a shave, and that's when my mother promised to smack the black off of him.

First things were first when we landed.

A car pulled up and my mother wanted to drop her bags and go shopping. Toy had scheduled a meeting with a public relations firm that wanted to pitch everything they could do for us, so I ended up getting my mother another limo so she could go shopping solo and have the car with her at all times.

My nervousness didn't calm down though, but I felt

good that I was the first high school player to make the jump to the European league since the NBA decided that high school players needed one year of college.

Jalen wasn't lying when he told me that Tori was keeping me on ice. I tried to call then text her, but she wasn't getting back.

Toy hadn't moved from in front of the television and *SportsCenter* since we returned from our meeting. I felt him looking at me when I was staring out the window, checking out NYC.

"You still thinking about your girl, *L*?"

Before I could answer, he was already putting his two cents in my personal.

"Don't worry about it. I'm telling you, after this draft and she hears all about it and all that money you're going to make, she'll be blowing your cell phone up."

Jalen was sitting on the couch, shuffling a deck of cards on a table. "What makes you think that?"

Toy exhaled. He and Jalen had been going back and forth on the simplest of things.

"I think it 'cause I know it. Women love money, and there is no way that little girl is going to let *L* walk away from her and keep her ass living up in The Vil."

"See, what you don't know, though, Tori ain't like that. And for all it's worth, *L*, I'm worried 'bout y'all getting back together, 'cause this ain't like Tori, man. Even though she told me how she was going to play you. It's just been too many days now. You know how we do it. We a family."

Toy stopped watching the TV when they started talking tennis. "Look, all the same, she's just trying to play you, so she can get more on the back end."

"Check this here, Toy," Jalen told him. "She's not worried about no back end, okay. Tori's not even like that. She came up with us and is the best thing for him. She's his friend too, a road dog for real. Like I say, family."

"Whatever you say, playa. But I'm telling you, ain't no

skank from The Vil going to turn down what L is offering. So shuffle that in your deck."

"Watch your mouth, Toy. I already told you she's family. Respect her!"

At that point I didn't think I needed to add any more 'cause now Toy was talking about my girl like he didn't care how I felt about her.

"Look, I'm getting a case listening to you trying to correct me," Toy told Jalen.

"And I'm tired of you disrespecting people you don't know."

"You mean like that ho the other day?"

Toy laughed and turned back around at the television, unaware that the small glass Jalen had picked up was headed in his direction. It hit the back of his chair and exploded, barely missing him.

Toy jumped out his seat and looked at the glass on the floor. "Oh, so you finally want to do this?"

"Punk, I been ready."

Jalen took a few steps to get closer, and Toy was already rolling up the sleeves of his shirt.

"Yeah, come on over here, so I can knock your ass out. First, you draw that pistol on me and don't use it, you put my business with L in jeopardy with your wannabe-thug-ass, money-making schemes, and now this? Yeah, c'mon over here and get knocked out."

I stepped right between them before they went to blows. "Would y'all fools sit down. Sit down and chill, Toy. You don't have to worry about my girl. And, Jalen, stop worrying about him talking about Tori. I got that, a'ight. I got it."

Chapter Twenty-seven

Time to Choose

Finally it was draft day. *Big, baby!*

There was so much media coverage, the hotel had to open up two conference rooms to accommodate everyone. And many fans came out, some of whom had never seen me play, except some of the clips on *SportsCenter*. The attention was so powerful, a few times I'd wished I was back in The Vil, on the court, in my own comfortable surroundings.

The rumors about all types of trades the teams in the league were making didn't help my nerves. Toy was getting word that Barcelona had changed their mind about making me their first pick, and sixth overall, opting for a big man instead. To get that number one spot, Olympiakos, a Greek team, for next year's number one draft pick, plus some cash, offered Barcelona their second selection first-round spot, leaving me out in the cold, not knowing what team, if any, was going to pick me up.

Then through all the swirls, Toy asked me to meet him out in the hall. He didn't hesitate. "We got trouble, *L*."

I looked at Jalen then back at Toy. "What kind of trouble?"

"Barcelona has definitely changed their mind and wants a big man now."

My whole life stopped right then and there. I felt like I couldn't get enough air. I just remember putting my hands up to my head for a second or two, trying to get my composure.

Jalen lashed out with the quickness. "And why they change their mind all of a sudden?"

"Look, they said they really like you," Toy explained.

"Okay, they like me, but they not sold on me right before they supposed to take me?"

"It's political," Toy responded.

"What the hell you mean, Toy?" Jalen asked.

"The league pushing their buttons, telling them, if they take you number one, they might not let them do any deals within the league for the next ten years."

"So what happens now? I mean, am I here for nothing, Toy?"

"Well, we go in there, sit down, and wait and see what happens. That's all we can do. If worse comes to worse, you can go to the B league and tear it up for one season then get in the league, like you planned all along."

"So what? No shoe deal?" Jalen sang. "His deal is for playing pro, not semi-pro."

"Toy, if I don't get taken, I have to pay New Funk back. You telling me I already spent money I don't have? If I don't get taken, I'm going to be right back in The Vil."

Toy looked in the direction of the huge conference room filled with media cameras and reporters then back at me without a word. From all appearances, it didn't seem like the news was all new to him.

"How long have you known about this, Toy?"

Toy looked at me with surprise. "What?"

Jalen himself wanted to know. "How long have you known about how they feeling?"

Toy looked us over. "Shit! A little over a week now. I thought things would work out on their own."

Without warning, Jalen reached over and punched Toy in the jaw. I tried to break them up, and two security guards came over and told us all to go sit down.

I sat down feeling like a fool for giving up my college eligibility, especially now since Tori didn't want anything to do with me. I was sitting there watching the draft on a big screen, not knowing whether I was getting a chance or not.

I looked over at my mom, who didn't know anything about what was going on, yet she had the proudest smile on her face. How was I going to tell her that we would have to move back to The Vil?

Meanwhile, Toy and Jalen were still beefing with their eyes.

After a few picks went by, my mother asked me why my name wasn't called. Then two more picks went by. She tugged on Toy's arm and asked him the same thing.

I felt embarrassed and ashamed that I'd made the wrong decision. As I sank down into my chair, all of a sudden, my name flashed across the big screen. With the fifth pick of the first round, LE MANS of France made me their number one pick!

Things turned out for the good and there was no way I had any complaints to going to France to play some ball. Right after the news and a few interviews with some reporters, we were in a black SUV with all the tricks back to the airport on our way back to Columbus, with a two-year, ten-million-dollar offer plus a signing bonus that was going to be kept on the hush.

Big, baby!

Chapter Twenty-eight

Picture Me Rolling

We rolled back into town feeling good and ready to finish up everything we had to do before I had to report to rookies camp in France. *France? France?* It was unbelievable.

Jalen was driving then stopped the Escalade. He seemed to have his focus back.

"I can't believe how fast they put this court up! Man, look at this!"

We were both giving each other hugs and pounds then shooting without a ball, like we did when we were young bucks on the come-up.

"They did a good job, J."

"Yup, and we're going to use them for the rec center too." Jalen jotted down something in his small notebook. "They putting up bleachers, right?"

"Yeah, we got enough for both sides, so when the tournament pop off, everybody is going to have a place to sit."

Jalen was looking around. "How many we tryin' to sit though?"

"Fifteen hundred," I told him. "Do it big."

Jalen pulled out his notebook again and started writing.

"Oh, so you takin' notes on everything, I see."

"Believe it. Yo', man, New York City ain't no joke. They 'bout business up in there, so I need to have mine on point."

"That's what I know, J. We on another level now."

"While you in that summer league, I signed up for a few summer courses in France."

"J, you don't speak no French, *negro*."

"They say they got American instructors for some of the classes. I bet when we leave there I'm going to know what to say when I whisper in a French cutie's ear. Everything is in place, man. We've done it! We're on our way!"

"Naah, man, not yet."

"Tori, right?"

"She's still not returning my calls."

"I talked to her this morning. It's going to be okay."

I think Jalen was still thinking that we were just having a little spat or whatnot and we would more than likely get back together. But I had different feelings altogether. Time was playing against me.

"So she okay?"

"That baby, man. It's messing her head up, not knowing what to do. Nobody need to be goin' through that, *L*."

"Hook up a dinner for me," I told him.

Jalen smiled. "Dinner?"

"Yeah. Tell her that I had to fly to France ahead of you, but you want to see her before we leave. When she walks in and sees me, she's going to have no choice but to talk, right?"

Jalen hooked the dinner up at the Brownstone Restaurant downtown. It was Friday night, so of course, it was packed with the crowd coming in for drinks and dinner after work.

Jalen had talked to the manager and told him I was coming out, so they put us in VIP, where we sat and waited.

Tori called Jalen and told him to meet her on the first level, and when he went down to get her, I felt like I was about to meet her for the first time. He was walking behind her when they made it back upstairs, and when he pointed to where we were sitting and she saw me, she stopped then looked back at him.

He grabbed her by the waist and sort of scooted her over to our table. Then they sat down.

"Now isn't this special?" he said.

"What's up, baby?" I was really happy to see her, even though she didn't have a smile on her face.

"Hey, *L*," she said, super-duper quick.

Jalen flipped over his BlackBerry. "Damn it!"

Tori looked over at him. "What's wrong?"

"That's the team in France. Gotta take this call. I'll probably be about an hour or a little longer."

"Dang! That long?" Tori sang. "I know you lying, *J*."

"I'm for real. 'Bout an hour, girl. The last time I talked to them, it took me forty-five minutes just to understand they were just saying hi!" Jalen kissed Tori on the cheek. "Gotta go."

Tori rolled her eyes at Jalen, and we sat at the table just looking at one another, halfway snacking on some breadsticks, sipping water, and listening to the music.

Tori stood up to leave.

I reached over for her. "Hold up. Where you goin'? I thought we were having some dinner?"

"No. I thought I was having dinner with Jalen."

"Tori, c'mon, we better than this. Can we at least talk?"

"Talk?"

"Yeah."

"About what?"

"You know . . . about things going on with you."

"Oh, I thought you wanted to talk about why you snuck off with that trick, Katrina."

"Look, I know that was a mistake. I mean, who don't make them?"

"Not mistakes like that. Katrina couldn't wait to rub that all in my face. Do you know what people are saying about me?"

I honestly didn't know, so I didn't answer her.

"They're saying I don't care, that as long as you're making money, I'm going to be with you, and I'm going to let you walk all over me."

"When did you start caring about what people say about you, Tori? Damn! You were the only virgin at"—I stopped myself as quick as I could because of what happened to her.

"No, go ahead," Tori pushed.

"You know what I mean."

"Yes, I do. Before I was raped, I was a virgin, and then I was raped and now have a baby inside me."

There wasn't anything I could say. Tori had way more problems to deal with than I did. I decided to tell her how I felt.

"I still want to get married."

"I don't understand why you would want to do that."

"You really don't know?"

Tori shook her head no, looking down at her glass of water.

"I want to marry you, Tori, because you're supposed to be the one I'm with."

When Tori looked at me, her facial expression wasn't hard anymore. It was like she enjoyed what I said but didn't really believe it.

"Girl, I'm serious. How many years have we talked about getting married? How many conversations have we had? How many plans have we made?"

"Yeah, we did all that."

"So what's the problem?"

"We didn't think I would be gang-raped and have a baby on the way though."

"But, see, the thing is, I'm willing to look past all that. Wasn't your fault in the first place, and if I knew who did this to you, they wouldn't be breathing. And that's my word."

Tori began to open up, and we started talking like we always had. We ordered steak, baked potatoes, and salad then dessert.

While we were eating, Tori told me that she'd made up her mind and planned to have an abortion the very next day but was so unsure about how it made her feel.

I let her know that whatever she wanted to do was fine with me, but the bottom line was, I wanted her to go with me to France so we could get married like we'd planned all along.

"I don't think that will work," she said.

"Why?"

"'Cause, L, it's just not. You'll be on the road, and there will be a lot of temptations. How are you going to resist it?"

"I will. It's something I'll have to do."

Tori didn't look like I was convincing her.

"Look, I won't be the only one on the team married. I just don't feel like dealing with groupies and all that. I want to be with you and spend all my time with you and concentrate on my game so it will be on fire once I jump to the league. Look, all I want to do is take care of you. That's all I want to do."

"Really? Take care of me and respect me?"

"Yes, baby, that's all I want to do. Me and you in France."

"And Jalen," she said.

"Yeah, and J."

Tori smiled a bit. I knew she was thinking of us getting out of Columbus and just starting fresh and doing what we had always planned.

She finally took my hand. "Sorry, L, I don't think so. I'm staying here. I just can't."

After Jalen came back, and we dropped Tori off. I watched her walk into her mother's spot in The Vil. I knew it was probably the last time I would see her for a long time. When she shut the door, I took out the ring I bought for her in New York and looked at it. Then put it back in my pocket.

"So what's next?" Jalen asked.

"Look, man, I tried. She's not hearing me. In a couple of days I have to dedicate the court to the streets, and then we're gone."

"Damn, man!" Jalen mumbled as he drove off. "Don't make no sense. Just don't make no damn sense."

Chapter Twenty-nine

Wake Up

I sat around trying to decide whether or not to go see Tori before it was too late. I went as far as to call Jalen so he could take me, but he didn't answer. I took that as a sign to just let things be. Plus, I didn't want to upset Tori anymore than she was, because she had planned to have the abortion in the morning. I ended up falling asleep.

Next thing I knew, my mother was pushing me on the shoulder. "L, you need to get up," she kept telling me.

I looked over at the clock. It was a little past three in the morning. "Ma, you all right?"

"Get up, L. We need to go to the hospital," she said, her voice trembling.

I tried to sit up in the bed. "Hospital? For what?"

"It's Jalen, baby. Something happened, and he's in the hospital."

I jumped out the bed and scurried to put on my clothes without even asking my mother what had happened. Out of all the money I had made in the last couple of weeks, I still didn't have a car, so we had to wait for a cab to pick us up and take us to Jalen.

When we got there, he was in intensive care. The doctor told us he was lucky to be alive in his condition. It was crazy because the same nurse who'd he met when he was in the hospital and who starred in his wild movie was standing by his bed, checking his chart.

I stepped inside.

She tried to smile at me, but a tear dropped down her brown face.

"What happened?"

"He was beaten up," she said.

"What? By who? For what?"

"I don't know. I have never seen anything like this though, and J is so sweet. You're Langston, right?"

I nodded yes.

"He called out for you a few minutes ago. He's going in and out."

Before I could ask another question, she ran out the room.

My mother came over to stand next to me and put her arm around me. We tried to call out for Jalen a few times, but he wouldn't answer. It was dark in the room. Jalen's face was covered with bandages, and he was motionless. I just started calling out to him over and over again.

When my mother ran out the room, I stood silent and looked down at Jalen, not knowing what else to do.

"*L, that you?*"

Jalen's worn out voice scared me. I leaned down toward his face. "*J, it's me. I'm right here. I'm right here, man.*" I was about to lose it.

"I'm fucked up, ain't I?"

"No, man, you a soldier. You goin' to be okay. You're good, man."

"Take a good look at me, *L.*"

"I am looking at you, Jalen. You're going to be okay. Just relax."

"No, *L,*" he said. "Take a good look. That nigga took off my arm and leg."

I pulled back the covers on Jalen's body, and my eyes cut through the darkness. I saw that his left leg and right arm were completely gone. Instantly my hands started to shake as I held the cover. I wanted to throw up and cry at the same time.

"Jalen, who did this to you, man? Who did it, gotdamn it?"

Jalen didn't answer me right away. He was back out.

I bent down and put my head on his chest and began to cry. My tears couldn't stop flowing. "Jalen, please . . . tell me who did this to you."

I heard Jalen trying to speak. Then he whispered, "Toy."

"Toy?"

"I was riding through The Vil."

Jalen's voice was so faint, I had to put my ear next to his mouth just to hear him.

He continued with, "Toy pinned me in with his car, jumped me with some crew. They beat me, and he told me if I didn't have my arm and leg, it would be hard for me to keep up with you when we go to France."

"He said that? He did this?"

"And he raped Tori, L. That bastard did that too."

"Tori?"

"He said her baby is probably his. He said he was on top of her for hours. He is the one who had her raped."

It was the first time in my life that I felt my mind totally snap. My whole body was boiling, and I was in shock.

I tried to tell Jalen that he would be okay, but I couldn't speak anymore. All I could do was look down at him as he fell back to sleep. I bent down and kissed him on the cheek and headed out to the streets.

When I reached the exit of the hospital, I heard my mother calling out to me, "Langston, where are you going?"

I didn't answer. I looked at her, kissed her on the forehead, then just started walking away as she continued to call out my name.

Chapter Thirty

Get-Back

I was walking through the streets in the darkness like a zombie. I was sweating, my tee was soaked, and my heart was pounding with straight fire. Probably out of force of habit, I stopped in The Vil. It was quiet on the street, except for a few drug dealers on the prowl, along with a few young bucks who should have been at home and tucked in bed.

I got an adrenaline surge when I saw Jalen's Escalade zoom right past me. Then the brake lights came on, and the car stopped. Like a bunch of magnets, the few people left on the street all gathered around to see who was in it.

I wanted to know too, so I stood and watched for a minute. Then I walked up slow. There was one young buck on a bike holding himself up by gripping the car door and talking to the driver, and two or three others walking around, checking out the rims Jalen had just put on his ride.

When I got up to the car, I took the young one hanging on the door by his arm and threw his ass off the car and onto the ground.

The punk driving Jalen's whip looked out. "Yo', man, what is your problem?" he said. Then when he saw my face, he said, "What's up, *L*?

I didn't know this fool who'd made himself comfortable in Jalen's wheels. "Where'd you get the whip?"

He answered, "Huh?"

I punched him in the face and snatched his ass through the car window then drug him on the pavement. I lifted him up in the air. "The car, where did you get it?"

"C'mon, *L*. I don't know, man. It was sitting down by Maryland pool. I walk by, look in, the music on, nobody in it, but the keys, so I take off."

"That's all you know?"

"That's it, man. I swear to you," he pleaded.

I looked back at the crew looking at me. "Y'all need to get your young asses out the streets. Go home! Go!"

They all took off running, except for the fool I had just yanked out. I kept my eye on him and got into Jalen's car.

"Hold up, man. I just bought a chicken meal. I ain't even bust it open yet," he said.

I looked over in the passenger seat and saw his food. I dropped his smoking-hot three-piece on the ground piece by piece, kept the drink, and drove off.

The shock of seeing Jalen was wearing me down. I just wanted to cry, but my anger kept me going. I wanted revenge. I had a feeling Jalen didn't get rid of his tool like I told him, because he didn't trust the streets. He knew someday for some reason he was going to need to use it to protect himself.

I reached under the seat and found his piece and began to think that he must have really been surprised by the fools that jumped out on him because he didn't get a chance to reach for it. Now I had his pistol and was going to make it right as soon as I could.

When I pulled up to Toy's house, I tucked the pistol in my pants and knocked on the door a few times. Without any questions, I was planning to blow his face off as soon as I saw him, but he never answered the door, and his car wasn't out front.

I drove over to The Strip Club, and sure enough, I spotted his ride. I got there just in time because just as I parked far enough away so that he couldn't see me, he came out the club holding Katrina by the arm.

"C'mon, bitch, get in the car," he was telling her.

"If you don't get off me, Toy," Katrina said. "Why you always have to be pushing on me?"

"What the hell your stupid ass going to do about it?" he barked.

"I wanna go home, Toy. I'm tired. I been dancing all night."

"You can walk your ass home from my place when I'm finished, so get your ass in the car."

"No, I wanna go home."

Toy smacked her.

I was on my way out the car, but my phone rang. "Yeah?" I answered it as Toy and Katrina struggled.

"Hey, baby. It's your mom."

"Hello, Ma."

By this time, Toy had pushed Katrina in the car and was on his way to the driver's side to get in.

"Langston . . . Jalen's dead, baby. He just passed away."

I could hear my mother crying on the phone. When I finally opened my eyes from the pain, Toy and Katrina were gone.

Chapter Thirty-one
Shed So Many Tears

Jalen's funeral wasn't my first, but it was my worst. I was barely coping with anything that had to do with life. My boy, who I'd been with every day since I could remember, was gone.

I went to the wake and cried until my eyes hurt. Jalen's mother didn't want an open casket, and I was glad. I wanted to think of only the good memories of him, but it was going to be hard to do after the way I saw him laying up in that hospital bed the night he was beaten.

Everyone gathered in Jalen's spot in The Vil, and people were running in and out bringing food and telling his mother how sorry they were. Most of the people who came through were parents who had lost kids in The Vil over some senseless nonsense too, so they knew exactly what to say to Jalen's mom.

It hurt me to see Jalen's mom try to deal with him being gone. Jalen's crazy ass was the first of her seven kids to graduate from high school, and he was her last born.

She was trying her best to be strong even as she tried to explain to Jalen's locked-up father what happened to his seed. She had no idea who killed Jalen. The police didn't know when they came out to talk to her, and they did their investigation like they barely cared.

I decided I was going to keep everything Jalen told me to myself and finish what I planned to do the night he died, because that was my boy, and I owed him.

I sat with Jalen's mom for a long while and tried to ease her pain, letting her know I would continue to pay Jalen's salary. It was the least I could do. After all, he was one of the main reasons I was going pro.

Jalen's mom told me to take his car though; she didn't think she could stay strong with it in her face every day and Jalen not driving it with his wide smile, and hat cocked to the side .

I was tired of everyone coming up to me asking how I was. Jalen didn't deserve to get beaten to death and have his arm and leg taken from him in the process.

When Jalen's mom heard someone ask me if I was okay again, she began to cry out. It was her third time within thirty minutes. Her daughters gathered her up and started to take her to her room.

Another tear rolled down my face as I looked at a picture of me and J washing our raggedy hand-me-down bikes with a rag and a bucket with holes.

I looked up from the picture when the front door opened and Tori walked in. She looked around at everyone then heard Jalen's mother crying out, and after one look into my eyes, she began to cry.

I stood up to grab her, and she fell into my arms. I started shedding tears again for Jalen. *Damn! Our boy is gone. Damn! He is gone.*

Every funeral I had ever been to had rained, and Jalen's was no different. I watched from a distance though from the backseat of one of the limos as they got ready to put J in the ground after the service. I didn't want to see him going down into the earth, nor did I want to hear any more crying because I think I would have had some kind of breakdown if I did.

We hadn't been at the cemetery more than five minutes, but I saw Tori looking around then back at the car. She came toward me with her umbrella, and I opened the door so she could get inside. She sat down and wiped a few drops from her face, as we sat in silence looking on at what was going on outside.

"You're not coming out, huh?"

"Naah, I've had enough. Jalen already in heaven anyway," I told her.

"Yeah?" Tori wondered.

"Probably already trying to get a summer b-ball tournament set up or something."

"You know his ass is. Probably trying to play a game of one on one with Jesus, with his crazy self."

I swear, I wasn't trying to cry again. "That was my boy, Tori. Jalen was my brother."

She said, "I loved him too. You just not supposed to go out like that, L."

I moved toward the window and looked out. I couldn't believe Toy had the nerve to be in attendance at Jalen's funeral. I don't know how long I stared at him, but I know I was thinking whether or not to go out there and kill him on the spot.

"What's wrong?" Tori asked.

"Nothing. I'm cool." I took a deep breath. I needed to talk about something else. Anything. "So how did it go?"

"What?"

I looked down at her stomach.

She hesitated before saying, "Oh, it didn't. I couldn't do it."

"No?"

"I couldn't." She exhaled loudly. "I mean, like you said, so what the baby won't know its father? How many kids in the hood know them anyway? Plus, this baby is going to have all of me inside it anyway. I promise you that."

I pounded my fist on my leg.

"What's wrong, L?"

"It seems like everything that's happened comes from me and going pro."

"What do you mean by that?"

"It don't matter. Just know that it's fucked-up to lose your best friend and girl in the same week."

"Well, I've been thinking about that too," Tori said.

"What you mean?"

"Just wondering what would happen if we just moved on, got away from here, and just did us."

"Really?"

"Mmm-mmm, you sit around and dream as a little girl of one day not having to live in the projects anymore and having a man with a family that you can cling to. Yeah, I thought about it."

"Yeah?"

"Yeah."

"And you were thinking about me?"

"Of course, I was."

I took my time before I spoke again. "You should do more than think about it though. You and the baby come with me. We'll get married and leave all this behind. No more projects, no more guns, no more murders. Just us and that little one inside you."

"But it's not yours, Langston. This baby won't be your blood."

"It will still be mine. I'll love it to death because it's part of you, and that's on my word."

Tori started to smile.

"So you'll do it? Oh, hold on a second." I reached into my pocket and gave her the ring I was still holding on to.

Tori's smile widened some more.

"You will?"

"Yes, boy, I'll marry you. Ain't no way I'm staying here without you."

Tori gave me a hug then a long kiss afterwards. I could see through the window they were finally lowering Jalen into the ground, and people were beginning to walk away.

"You see, Jalen. We're going to do it, baby! Me and your girl going to get married, man." I looked at Tori. "You know we should name the baby *Jalen*."

"And if it's a girl, *Jada*."

"Yeah, cool. I like that."

We both had tears running down our faces. I wiped mine away. "Now c'mon. Let's go say one last good-bye to our boy." I grabbed a bottle of liquor from the limo to share with Jalen and showed it to Tori. "You think J would like this? It's Johnnie Walker Blue Label."

"Oh, hell yeah. Jalen would drink anything."

I helped Tori out the limo, and we walked hand in hand to Jalen's grave then had our own little private time with our boy without shedding another tear.

Chapter Thirty-two

This on Me

I felt good knowing that Tori was going with me to France, but I still had to deal with Toy. I had let him breathe long enough.

I called him up. When he answered, his voice never before seemed so fake to me. It only made me wonder how many other people he had killed.

"We need to meet," I told him.

"Yeah? What's up?"

"Been thinking about those investments you talked about. I think I want to do a few. I want to sign on before I leave."

"Yeah?"

"That's right."

"So what made you change your mind?"

"Life, man, just life. You have to get it while it's good, right?"

"No doubt. Look, I was going to reach out to you about your boy, but I thought I would let you get through it awhile. Another senseless murder in the hood, you know."

I could tell he was trying to feel me out. "Yeah, you got that right."

"A'ight," he said. "Call me when you ready to meet."

"I will."

"The sooner the better," Toy said.

When I hung up the phone, my mother was standing near the sink, getting a glass of water.

"So what are you signing with Toy?" she asked.

"A few investments, that's all."

"Anything you want me to look at for you?"

"Naah, they all good. Just some property downtown and stuff like that."

I sat down at the kitchen table with her. She was still shaken by Jalen's death and had been going back and forth visiting his mother. I was wondering what I was going to do to Toy and how, and whether I could get away with it or not.

"What's wrong, L?"

" Oh, nothing. I just want to give you all my information on my accounts so that you can go in and get my money if anything ever happens to me."

My mother was quick. "Happen to you? Like what?"

"I don't know. I mean, like Jalen . . . if I ever get killed or something."

"Boy, ain't nothing going to happen to you. You're a chosen one."

"You never know, Ma. "

"What's gotten into you? Now you know I'm not going to be able to stand it if you don't have your faith. You're getting ready to travel all over the world playing ball, and you're going to need your faith and confidence sky-high all the time."

"I know, but you still need it, just in case."

The court was finally finished. The contractor that Jalen worked with to get the whole thing together called and let me know that they were putting up the nets on the rims and wanted me to come down to see how it looked with the bleachers because the kids were dying to bounce up and down on the new rubber matted pavement he'd laid down. He seemed really down concerning Jalen, telling me that Jalen was one young man on the move who just needed a little more seasoning and would have turned into a fine businessman.

When we finally pulled up to the court, there were about fifty kids and a few parents standing around the court looking at the painting of Jalen that me and the contractor decided to put on the center of the court. When they saw me get out the car with Tori, they all cheered.

We walked to the middle of the court, dedicated it to Jalen, and begged them to always come to the court to have fun, without the violence. All of a sudden, a big truck pulled up, opened up the back doors, and basketballs were being thrown to the court, sending the kids wild.

"Aww! This is so nice, *L*," Tori said.

"Yeah, they need this. Keep them off the corners, turning them drugs, you know."

"And they get to remember Jalen too," Tori said.

We sat around in the bleachers watching the young'uns go buck wild on the court for a while.

Tori said, "You ever think they are going to get who killed Jalen?"

"I don't know, but I am," I told her.

"What?"

"Just what I said."

"You know, *L*?"

I didn't answer, but she read my eyes.

"How? I mean, what happened?"

"He told me, Tori. Jalen told me when I went to see him before he died."

"And you've been keeping this inside all this time?"

"I had to. Can't trust anybody around here. You know that."

"You can trust me. I'm gonna be your wife."

Just then, a ball bounced into the bleachers. I grabbed it and gave it to a little boy, who thanked me for having the court built.

Tori hadn't taken her eyes off of me. She wanted to know what I knew.

"It was Toy."

Her eyes began to well up. "Are you sure?"

"That's what he told me. I heard him clear as day."

Tori wiped a tear from her face.

"He told me something else, Tori."

"What was it?"

I waited a few seconds before I answered her. I felt myself biting my lip. "Jalen said Toy was the one who set you up to get raped. And it makes sense now, because he's the one who told us where we could find you."

Tori was silent for minutes. She looked out at the kids screaming and playing. She looked at me hard then said, "Are you going to need any help, baby?"

I looked back at her then back out at the kids standing around looking at the drawing of Jalen.

"Naah, you just get ready to go, okay. I got this. This all on me."

Chapter Thirty-three
Pop! Pop!

I was locked and loaded waiting outside The Strip Club for Toy. My heart was racing. I was a little nervous, but when I saw him walking out, the smile on his face filled me with mad get-back. I wondered if that was the way he looked when he walked away with Jalen lying in his own blood, or after having his moment with my girl.

Toy flopped down in Jalen's ride. "Young brother, the back rooms in the VIP are poppin' tonight," he said. "I mean, really getting buck wild." Then he looked around, probably remembering we were in J's ride. "Look, when we done with this, you need to come inside so we can really party."

"Not my thing," I told him.

"A'ight, whatever." Toy reached into his suit jacket and pulled out the paperwork and began to unfold it. "When you're an old man like me, *L*, you're going to be happy you did this."

I wasn't paying much attention to Toy because I was looking around the lot and at the vacant building next to the club. That's where I had planned on taking him and laying him out.

"So you ready for France or what? They told me they are starting you at shooting guard right out the gate. Just be careful 'cause those 'Euros' will bust your ass when you drive to the hole. I plan on traveling there to check things out and meet your coach in a couple of days, maybe even get me a spot."

I was really tired of hearing his voice. "Yeah, whatever, Toy."

He looked up from the papers. "Whatever? C'mon, what do you mean? This is our—"

I snatched the papers from his hand and threw them to the floor. "Why'd you do it?"

His lying eyes wandered around. "Do what?"

"So now you're a killer and a liar?"

"Killer? What the hell you talkin' about?"

I locked the car doors then pulled the pistol from up under my tee. "Jalen. That's what I'm talking about."

Toy kind of laughed.

I snapped at his arrogance and put the gun right on his temple. "Shut up! And you raped Tori too!"

Toy had his hands up and was looking at the pistol I was trying to push through his head. "L, c'mon, man. I think you got some bad information or something."

"Info came from J's mouth while he was on his death bed."

Toy stuttered, "W-w-well, he was lying to you. I know that much. C'mon, get the tool off my head."

"Shut up, Toy. You had some thugs snatch Tori up, and you gang-raped her then told me where she was when you were sure I would sign with your crooked ass."

"Rape? I ain't never raped anybody in my life. Now, c'mon. Put the gun down, so we can talk about this shit like real men. We got too much at stake for this here."

I wasn't in the mood for his cons and pleas. Jalen wouldn't lie to me, and Toy looked guilty.

I looked around the lot and made sure it was empty then unlocked the door. "Get out."

"What?"

"Get out, Toy."

As Toy stepped out the car, I kept my pistol on him. I walked over to his side of Jalen's ride.

Toy probably saw the fear on my face and tried to get cocky. "Now what? You goin' to shoot me right here? Young'un, you don't have the guts."

Out of the darkness, a female voice said, "But I do."

I looked through the night to see who it was. It was Katrina. She walked up to Toy. Her face was swollen, and I could see blood dripping from her mouth.

Katrina said, "I bet you and your friends don't rape me or anybody else again."

Before Toy could say one word, Katrina lifted up her arm and fired two shots from the pistol she was holding. We stood still; looking at him lay in his own foul blood.

Katrina wiped her bloody mouth, spit on Toy then looked at me. "We gonna just let him lay there, *L*?"

Toy was dead. There was no denying that. I wasn't sure how I felt about it, but I felt better for Tori, Jalen, and Katrina.

I tucked my tool under my tee and took a good look to make sure no one else was around and said to Katrina, "Yeah, why not? I didn't shoot him, and neither did you."

ORDER FORM
URBAN BOOKS, LLC
78 E. Industry Ct
Deer Park, NY 11729

Name: (please print):_____

Address: _____

City/State: _____

Zip: _____

QTY	TITLES	PRICE
	16 ½ On The Block	$14.95
	16 On The Block	$14.95
	Betrayal	$14.95
	Both Sides Of The Fence	$14.95
	Cheesecake And Teardrops	$14.95
	Denim Diaries	$14.95
	Happily Ever Now	$14.95
	Hell Has No Fury	$14.95
	If It Isn't love	$14.95
	Last Breath	$14.95
	Loving Dasia	$14.95
	Say It Ain't So	$14.95

Shipping and Handling - add $3.50 for 1st book then $1.75 for each additional book.

Please send a check payable to:

Urban Books, LLC

Please allow 4 - 6 weeks for delivery

ORDER FORM
URBAN BOOKS, LLC
78 E. Industry Ct
Deer Park, NY 11729

Name: (please print):_____

Address: _____

City/State: _____

Zip: _____

QTY	TITLES	PRICE
	The Cartel	$14.95
	The Cartel#2	$14.95
	The Dopeman's Wife	$14.95
	The Prada Plan	$14.95
	Gunz And Roses	$14.95
	Snow White	$14.95
	A Pimp's Life	$14.95
	Hush	$14.95
	Little Black Girl Lost 1	$14.95
	Little Black Girl Lost 2	$14.95
	Little Black Girl Lost 3	$14.95
	Little Black Girl Lost 4	$14.95

Shipping and Handling - add $3.50 for 1st book then $1.75 for each additional book.
Please send a check payable to:
Urban Books, LLC
Please allow 4 - 6 weeks for delivery

ORDER FORM
URBAN BOOKS, LLC
78 E. Industry Ct
Deer Park, NY 11729

Name: (please print):_____

Address: _____

City/State: _____

Zip: _____

QTY	TITLES	PRICE
	A Man's Worth	$14.95
	Abundant Rain	$14.95
	Battle Of Jericho	$14.95
	By The Grace Of God	$14.95
	Dance Into Destiny	$14.95
	Divorcing The Devil	$14.95
	Forsaken	$14.95
	Grace And Mercy	$14.95
	Guilty & Not Guilty Of Love	$14.95
	His Woman, His Wife His Widow	$14.95
	Illusion	$14.95
	The LoveChild	$14.95

Shipping and Handling - add $3.50 for 1st book then $1.75 for each additional book.
Please send a check payable to:
Urban Books, LLC
Please allow 4 - 6 weeks for delivery

ORDER FORM
URBAN BOOKS, LLC
78 E. Industry Ct
Deer Park, NY 11729

Name: (please print):_____

Address: _____

City/State: _____

Zip: _____

QTY	TITLES	PRICE

Shipping and Handling - add $3.50 for 1st book then $1.75 for each additional book.
Please send a check payable to:
Urban Books, LLC
Please allow 4 - 6 weeks for delivery

Notes

Notes